George G Vasey

English Grammar Made Easy

and adapted to the capacity of children - in which English accidence and

etymological parsing are rendered simple and attractive

George G Vasey

English Grammar Made Easy
and adapted to the capacity of children - in which English accidence and etymological parsing are rendered simple and attractive

ISBN/EAN: 9783337391997

Printed in Europe, USA, Canada, Australia, Japan

Cover: Foto ©Andreas Hilbeck / pixelio.de

More available books at **www.hansebooks.com**

LOVELL'S SERIES OF SCHOOL BOOKS.

ENGLISH

GRAMMAR MADE E

AND ADAPTED

THE CAPACITY OF CHIL

- IN WHICH

Montreal:
PUBLISHED BY JOHN LOVELL;
OLD BY R. & A. MILLER.

Toronto:
LLER, 87 YONGE STREET.
1860.

PREFACE.

Children, in general, have an aversion to Grammar. Their universal complaints are that it is difficult,—that it is disagreeable,—that, in fact, they cannot understand it. We sincerely feel and acknowledge the justness of these complaints.

At the same time, we are fully convinced that the cause of these obstructions does not exist so much in the subject of Grammar itself, as in the manner in which the subject has been treated. Although we have examined upwards of thirty different English Grammars, we have not seen one adapted to the capacity of children : they are all decidedly too technical, even in their very first lessons, and consequently too abstruse for the use of children. They demand an amount of knowledge in children of seven or eight years, which is rarely possessed by youths of twelve or fourteen.*

It is very important that children should commence their grammatical studies early. Vulgarisms and other improprieties of speech, as well as imperfections in Orthography and Syntax, when once acquired, are very tenacious, and can never be thoroughly eradicated.

It is, therefore, highly desirable that an elementary book on English Grammar, at once easy and interesting, should be placed in the hands of our younger pupils : such a book is an important desideratum. It is confidently hoped that this desideratum will be adequately supplied by the present publication.

The simplicity and novelty of the plan upon which it is constructed, will be readily understood from the following summary.

---

* Two exceptions may be mentioned to this declaration, namely, Mrs. Marcet's very clever and interesting little work called *Mary's Grammar*, and a pictorial production called *The Play-Grammar*; but neither of these is at all adapted to the use of schools or of classes.

The work is divided into Three Parts.

PART FIRST

Commences with familiar explanations of the few grammatical terms which are absolutely necessary to be known in describing the Parts of Speech.

It then gives ample descriptions of the Parts of Speech in their simplest forms. Thus, the Noun is described as the name of every kind of visible object, *with many illustrations:* but no mention is made of abstract, or verbal, or collective Nouns; nor is any reference made to Gender, Number, or Case, nor even to the distinction of Proper and Common. All these modifications are reserved for the Second Part. An exercise is then added, which can be performed easily by any child of seven years, after two readings of the descriptions and illustrations, without any committing to memory.

The Adjective is described, with numerous illustrations; but no reference is made to Degrees of Comparison.

The Pronoun is described and illustrated; but no reference is made to Gender, Number, Person, or Case.

The Verb is explained in the simplest manner; but no reference is made to Number, Person, Moods, or Tenses.

The Adverbs are copiously illustrated; but no mention is made of Degrees of Comparison, or of Classification into Quality, Manner, Time, or Place.

And so on of the others; each Part of Speech being followed by appropriate Exercises.

PART SECOND

Describes and illustrates those Inflections and Modifications which are omitted in Part First. Part Second constitutes a complete *"Accidence"* of the English language.

Each Model-Conjugation of the Verbs is so arranged, that all its Moods and Tenses can be seen at one view, in a distinct and orderly manner.

PART THIRD

Contains:—1. Several familiar illustrations of the Parts of Speech. 2. Copious illustrations of *Etymological Parsing*, by which that operation is rendered simple and easy; with numerous exercises. 3. Analytical illustrations and observations for the special use of Teachers.

GRAMMAR MADE EASY.

PART FIRST.

Lesson I.

Speaking, Talking, or Language.

When we speak or talk, we use our breath and tongue to make sounds; these sounds are called *Words;* and all the words we make use of are called *Language.*

When we speak or talk to each other, we make use of language.

Letters and Words.

When we read in a book, we make use of signs or marks. These signs or marks are called *Letters.* When letters are properly placed together, they form *Words.* For example, *m* is a letter, *a* is a letter, and *n* is a letter: when we put them together in this manner—*man*, they form the word "man."

Now you see and understand that signs of language may be marked or printed, and made into books; so that we have two methods or ways of using language :

> *First,* — Spoken language.
> *Second,*—Printed language.

When we speak language, we make use of sounds only; but when we print language, we make use of various marks or signs, which we call *Letters*.

When two or more of these letters are placed together properly, they form or represent a word; for instance, if we place these three letters b o y together, they form the word *boy*.

What is a Sentence ?

When two or more words are placed together properly, so as to mean something, they form a phrase, or a sentence, or a speech; for example, if we take the following words—

you,	well,	have,	book,
this,	new,	learn,	lesson,
your,	will,	and,	

we may place them properly together so as to form a short speech, which we call a sentence, thus—

"Learn your lesson well, and you will have this new book."

There—that is a *Sentence*.

What is Grammar ?

When we are learning to put letters together to make words, or to put words together to make sentences, in a proper manner, *we are learning* GRAMMAR.

And when we are learning how to speak, and to read, and to write, in a proper manner, *we are learning* GRAMMAR.

Lesson II.

Grammar is divided into four parts; namely, Orthography, Etymology, Syntax, and Prosody.

ORTHOGRAPHY.

The FIRST PART of Grammar teaches *the proper method of putting letters together* to form words. This part of Grammar is called

ORTHOGRAPHY, or *the Art of Spelling Words.*

For example, if we put the letters *m a n* together, they spell *man;* if we put the letters *d o g* together, they spell *dog.* In the same way, *l a d* spells *lad,* and *m a d* spells *mad;* *l a n d* spells *land,* and *s a n d* spells *sand.*

This is ORTHOGRAPHY. *Orthography* is *correct spelling,* and *correct spelling* is *Orthography.*

ETYMOLOGY.

The SECOND PART of Grammar (which is called ETYMOLOGY) is divided into *three branches,* and teaches three things.

The *First Branch* of Etymology teaches the Classification of Words, or the *different kinds or sorts of words* : for example,

Some words mean *things;* as book, tree, water.

Some words mean *qualities;* as good, bad, idle.

Some words mean *actions;* as run, walk, jump.

The *First Branch* of Etymology teaches us to classify and arrange all these different sorts of words.

Parts of Speech.

When we speak, or make a *speech*, we use words, and each word we speak is a *part* of the speech ; and all the different kinds of words are called PARTS OF SPEECH.

The *First Branch* of Etymology teaches us to name and understand the different *Parts of Speech.*

The *Second Branch* of Etymology teaches *the changes which take place in words :* for instance, we use the word run, and we say, I *run ;* but when we use the word *he,* we say, he runs ; we say of a boy who often runs, that he is a run*ner ;* and when we see him run, we say he is run*ning.*

Thus, you see that the word *run* is changed into run*s,* run*ner,* run*ning.* So also *read* is changed to read*s,* read*er,* read*ing.*

The *Third Branch* of Etymology explains how one word comes from or grows out of another ; for example,

From	strong,	comes	strength ;
From	young,	comes	youth ;
From	high,	comes	height ;
From	frost,	comes	freeze.

Lesson III.

The SECOND PART of Grammar teaches three things ; namely,

1. The different kinds of words, or Parts of Speech.
2. The changes which are made in words.
3. How one word grows out of another.

These are the *three branches* of the second part of Grammar, which is called ETYMOLOGY.

SYNTAX.

The THIRD PART of Grammar explains to us *the proper way of putting words together* when we speak to each other, or write. When words are thus properly put together, so as to mean something which can be well understood, they make a phrase, or a speech, or a sentence.

This part of Grammar is called SYNTAX.

PROSODY.

The FOURTH PART of Grammar teaches us how to speak all our words and sentences, and give them their *proper sounds or pronunciation.*

This part of Grammar is called PROSODY.

The Four Parts of Grammar are called

1. Orthography.	3. Syntax.
2. Etymology.	4. Prosody.

REMARKS TO THE TEACHER.

[As this little book is intended only as an Easy Introduction to any of the Grammars in general use, it will be chiefly devoted to that part of Etymology which treats of the Classification of Words, namely, the Parts of Speech, or different sorts of words, and the changes they undergo.

ORTHOGRAPHY AND DERIVATION.

Orthography (though an essential and very important part of grammar) is usually taught in a separate book, called a Spelling-Book. The "Classical English Spelling-Book" has been prepared expressly to accompany the present "Grammar Made Easy."

The "Classical English Spelling-Book" contains a list of all the English monosyllables, arranged in classes, from the shortest to the longest monosyllables in the language; thus, beginning with words of two letters, and increasing gradually, according to the following order:

First step.—Me, be, he—so, no, go, &c.

Second step.—Man, pan—men, pen, &c.

Third step.—Hand, land—mend, send, &c.

Fourth step.—Stand, grand—blind, grind, &c.

Fifth step.—Strand, branch—blench, drench, &c.

Sixth step.—Thought, brought, draught, &c.

Seventh step.—Straight, strength, strengths.

Spelling Lessons in the irregular and difficult words, such as

once,   debt,   ache,   aisle,   drachm,

are introduced at intervals, according to the progress and intelligence of the pupil.

The graduated spelling-lessons are followed by several hundred Sentences on Equivocal Words and Verbal Distinctions.

The "Classical English Spelling-Book" also contains a very complete collection of Roots and Derivatives (Anglo-Saxon, Latin, and Greek), *with numerous "Illustrative Examples" as models for the use of Teachers and Parents.*

It likewise comprises Latin Mottoes and Quotations, English Proverbs and Maxims, Lists of Abbreviations, and all the concomitants of a first-rate Etymological Spelling-Book.]

Lesson IV.

CLASSIFICATION OF WORDS.

PARTS OF SPEECH.

The words of the English language are divided and arranged into nine classes, which are called the Nine Parts of Speech ; namely,

1. Noun.   4. Pronoun.   7. Preposition.
2. Adjective. 5. Verb.   8. Conjunction.
3. Article,   6. Adverb,   9. Interjection.

1.—NOUNS or NAMES.

A Noun is the name of any person, place, or thing.

Man, woman, child, John, Mary, Fred, are Nouns : they are the names of persons.

Montreal, Quebec, Toronto, are Nouns : they are the names of places.

Chair, hat, house, stone, hammer, nail, are Nouns : they are the names of things.

A Noun is the name of any beast, bird, fish, reptile, insect, or other animal.

Lion, tiger, wolf, eagle, pigeon, owl, are Nouns : they are the names of beasts and birds.

Shark, salmon, herring, crocodile, rattlesnake, are Nouns : they are the names of fishes and reptiles.

Wasps, hornets, musquitoes, are Nouns : they are the name of insects.

All names of persons are Nouns.
All names of places are Nouns.
All names of things are Nouns.

All names of beasts, birds, fishes, reptiles, and insects, are Nouns.

All the names of all other animals are Nouns.

A Noun's the name of any thing,
As *school* or *garden, hoop* or *swing.*

EXERCISES ON THE NOUNS.

The pupils must point-out the Nouns in the following sentences:

John saw a fish and a crab in the water.

Give me the pen and ink, and a sheet of paper.

The roof of that house has two chimnies on it.

There is a man carrying a ladder up the street.

Lock the door of that room, and give me the key.

The ship is on the sea, and the boat is on the river.

The dog has caught a rat, and the cat has caught a mouse.

My father has gone to town to-day, to buy a coat and hat.

Lions and elephants are found in Africa and in Asia.

[NOTE.—Many other words are Nouns, such as the names of employments, actions, states, feelings, &c.; but it would be premature to introduce such at this early stage; neither would it be judicious, at present, to trouble the child with the accidents of gender and case, or the formation of plurals.]

Lesson V.

2. — ADJECTIVES.

An Adjective is very different from a Noun. A Noun tells us the *name* of any thing: an Adjective tells us the *kind*, *sort*, or *quality* of any thing.

The word *sugar* is a Noun. There are several sorts of sugar.

There is *white* sugar and *brown* sugar.

There is *hard* sugar and *soft* sugar.

There is *dry* sugar and *moist* sugar.

There is *fine* sugar and *coarse* sugar.

There is *good* sugar and *bad* sugar.

All these little words, *white, brown, hard, soft, dry, moist, fine, coarse, good, bad*, tell us about the sort, or kind, or quality, of the sugar, and they are all called ADJECTIVES.

Every object or thing in the world is of some sort, or kind, or quality: for example, every boy is either *tall*, or *short*, or *clever*, or *stupid*, or *industrious*, or *idle ;* a house is either *large* or *small*, or *low* or *high ;* a table is either *wide* or *narrow*, or *round* or *square.*

The words *tall, short, clever, stupid, industrious, idle*, tell us the kind or sort of boy; the words *large, small, low, high*, tell us the kind or sort of house; the words *wide, narrow, round, square*, tell us the kind or sort of table.

All these words telling us the kind or sort, are called ADJECTIVES.

All the words which tell us of the kind, or sort, or quality, of anything in the world, are called ADJECTIVES.

The words which tell us of the number of any-thing are likewise called ADJECTIVES; as *one* apple, *two* oranges, *three* books.

The words which tell us of the order in which things are placed are also called ADJECTIVES; as, *first, second, third, fourth,* and so on.

Adjectives are words which tell us of the kind, or sort, or quality of any person, or animal, or thing; or the number and the order of persons, animals, or things.

> Adjectives tell the *kind* of Noun;
> As *great, small, pretty, white,* or *brown.*

EXERCISES ON THE ADJECTIVES.

The pupil must point-out the Adjectives in the fol-lowing sentences:

Little John saw a red rose in my good uncle's large garden.

Your round inkstand is standing on my square table.

I saw a pretty bird sitting on a high tree in the green lane.

My kind father bought me this beautiful book, because I am a diligent boy.

A hot day,—the bright sun,—a white cloud.

The day is hot, the sun is bright, and the clouds are white.

I have two brothers and three sisters.

James is the first, I am the second, Mary is the third, and Eliza is the fourth.

Lesson VI.

3. — ARTICLES.

An *Article* is a kind of Adjective which is placed before a Noun to show its particular meaning.

There are only two Articles in English,—

THE and AN.

(AN is frequently changed to A.)

The is called the Definite (or particular) Article, because it points-out some particular Noun.

An is called the Indefinite (or *not* particular) Article, because it does not point-out any particular Noun.

When we say, Give me *the* apple, we mean *some particular* apple that we have mentioned before ; but when we say, Give me *an* apple, we mean *any* apple, and not a particular one.

When we use the Indefinite Article (*an*) before a word beginning with a consonant, or full *h*, we leave out the *n ;* thus we say, *a* man, *a* house.

[NOTE.—*An* is the original Article from the Saxon. It was afterwards shortened or contracted into *a*. It is the same as the Adjective *one*, and corresponds exactly with the French Article *un*.]

EXERCISES ON THE ARTICLE.

Point-out the different kinds of Articles in the following sentences, and say why *a* or *an* is used :

Give me a sheet of paper, and the pencil I had yesterday. I have an orange, and John has an apple. Let us cross the river in a boat, and take a walk on the island.

An ape, an eagle, an ice-berg, an otter.

An honest man ; an honorable man ; an hospital.

Lesson VII.

4.—PRONOUNS.

Pronouns are words which are used instead of Nouns to prevent us from saying the some words over again.

For example, *The man* is clever, *the man* is useful ; *the man* is good, *the man* is happy Here the same words are repeated several times : but we may say, The man is clever, *he* is useful ; *he* is good, *he* is happy.

Here the word *he* is used instead of the *Noun* man ; and therefore the word *he* is a Pronoun.

The word *pro-noun* means *for a Noun.*

Let us take another example : " A *woman* went to a *man,* and the *woman* told the *man* that the *man* was in danger of being murdered by *robbers,* as the *robbers* were getting ready to attack the *man.* The *man* thanked the *woman* for the *woman's* kindness ; and as the *man* was not able to defend the *man's* self, the *man* left the *man's* house and went to a neighbour's."

This would be a very tiresome way of talking ; but by using Pronouns we can do it much better. We can say, " A woman went to a man, and *she* told *him* that he was in danger of being murdered by robbers, as *they* were getting ready to attack *him.* *He* thanked *her* for *her* kindness ; and as *he* was not able to defend *himself, he* left *his* house and went to a neighbour's."

The words *she, him, he, they, her, his, himself,* are all *Pronouns,* because they stand *for Nouns,* or *instead of Nouns.* They stand instead of the Nouns *man, woman,* and *robbers.*

The pupil must point-out the Pronouns in the following sentences:

Will you give me some apples? I do not know were they are. Here they are. Take them away. Give them to the cook, and tell her to make a pudding with them, and serve it up for dinner. Have you my pens or his? I have neither his nor yours; but you have mine.

Instead of Nouns the Pronouns stand,—
John's head, *his* face, *my* arm, *your* hand.

Lesson VIII.

5.—VERBS.

The master *teaches* John. James *beats* John.

The master *does something* to John,—he *teaches* him; James *does something* to John,—he *acts upon* him, he *beats* him.

When a word means *to do something*, and *to act upon something*, it is called a VERB; the words *teach*, *teaches*, *beat*, *beats*, are VERBS.

John is *taught*; he is *beaten*.

Here you see John is *acted upon; something is done* to him; he *suffers something*.

When a word means *to suffer something*, or *to be acted upon*, or *to be done to*, it is called a VERB; the words *taught* and *beaten* are VERBS.

I *am*, John *sits*, you *stand*.

When a word means *to be something*, it is called a VERB: the words *am*, *sits*, *stand*, are VERBS.

2

EXERCISES ON THE VERBS.

The pupil must point-out the Verbs in the following sentences :

The bird flies up into the tree, and hops from branch to branch.

I wrote a letter, and sent it to my friend.

I bought some good books, which I will give to the best boys.

Write your exercises, and bring them to me that I may correct them.

My father has built a house for us to live in.

Come in ; shut the door, and open the window.

James sits and reads ; John stands and talks.

Look at that frog ; see how it hops !

Cease to do evil, learn to do well.

Avoid bad company ; imitate good examples.

The girls run. The boys jump. I come, and you go. The ball rolls. James eats an apple. I dance. She sleeps. He plays.

Lesson IX.

6.—ADVERBS.

As Verbs tell us of things being done, so Adverbs tell us *how* the things are done ; as, *slowly*, *quickly*, *ill*, or *well*.

An Adverb is used to explain the quality or manner of Verbs and Adjectives. An Adverb also sometimes explains the kind and quality of another Adverb ; that is, one Adverb explains another Adverb.

When we say, the sun shines *brightly*, the word *brightly* tells us the manner of its shining.

When we say the ball rolls *rapidly*, the word *rapidly* tells the manner of its rolling.

Therefore these words *brightly* and *rapidly* are ADVERBS.

When we say, He reads *well*, here you see and understand that the word *well* explains to us *how* the reading is done,—it tells us the reading is *well* done. The Adverb *well* explains the quality and manner of the Verb *reads*.

When we say, He is a *good* man, the Adjective *good* tells us of the quality of the Noun *man;* it explains to us that the man has goodness, and does good. But when we say, he is a VERY *good* man, the Adverb *very* tells us of the kind or quality of the Adjective *good ;* it explains to us that the man not only has goodness, but that he has *much* goodness; and that he not only does good, but that he does *much* good. The Adverb *very* explains the kind and quantity of the Adjective *good.*

When we say, He reads VERY *correctly,* the Adverb *very* tells us of the kind or quality of the Adverb *correctly ;* it tells us that he reads with *much* correctness, or with *great* correctness. Here you see one Adverb explains another Adverb.

Adverbs explain or qualify Verbs.
Adverbs explain or qualify Adjectives.
Adverbs explain or qualify other Adverbs.

EXERCISES ON THE ADVERB.

The pupil must point-out the Adverbs in the following sentences :

The hare runs swiftly.   The girl sings sweetly.
The dog barks loudly.   Speak gently.
How fiercely the lion roars !
I am pretty well.   My brother is rather unwell.
He studies diligently.   I can draw tolerably well.

Lesson X.

7.—PREPOSITIONS.

A Preposition is a kind of word which we use to connect words with one another, and to show the relation between them.

If we say, John's hat is *on* his head, the word *on* points out to us, or shows us, the place or situation of the hat, in connection with the head; it shows us the relation of the hat to the head; it shows us how the hat and the head are placed together or joined.

In like manner, if we say, John's head is *under* his hat, the word *under* points out to us, or shows us, the situation of the head in connection with the hat; it shows us the relation of the head to the hat; it shows us how the head and hat are placed together or joined.

When we say, his hat is *on* his head, we understand that his hat is *over* or *upon* or *above* his head.

When we say, his head is *under* his hat, we understand that his head is *below* his hat. These words show the *relation* between the hat and the head; they show how the hat and the head are related to each other.

      John's hat is *on* his head.
      John's head is *under* his hat.

Words which show the relation or situation of persons or things (either Nouns or Pronouns) are called PREPOSITIONS.

If we say, John holds his hat *in* his hand, the word *in* shows the relation between the hat and the hand.

Again :—He took his hat *up* stairs.

He put it *under* the bed.

He placed it *behind* the table.

He threw it *over* the wall.

He let it drop *into* the river.

He took it *out-of* the water.

He hung it *before* the fire.

These words *up, under, behind, over, into, before, out-of*, all show the situation of the hat ; they tell us *where* the hat was placed, or where it was taken to. They are all PREPOSITIONS.

———

EXERCISES ON THE PREPOSITIONS.

The pupil must point-out the Prepositions in the following sentences :

My father and sister are within the house.

You may go with me, but I can go without you.

My uncle has gone into the country.

I went from Montreal to Quebec by water.

This is the house of my friend.

He passed through the avenue between the trees.

He was standing beneath the tree near the gate.

I am living at Ottawa, down near the river.

The dog went away after his master, but came back before him.

Lesson XI.

8.—CONJUNCTIONS.

Conjunctions join words and sentences together.
For example:

Two *and* three are five.
John is healthy *because* he is temperate.
I will go *if* you will go with me.
He labors harder *than* I do.
John came with me, *but* went away without me.

Here you see the words *and, because, if, than,
but,* are used to connect or join together words
and sentences, and parts of sentences.

These words *and, because, if, than, but,* are
called CONJUNCTIONS.

The word *Conjunction* means *a joining together.*

9.—INTERJECTIONS.

Interjections are words which we often make
use of when we feel any sudden pain, or great
pleasure; when we are very much surprised, or
astonished, or disgusted.

Oh! O fie! Oh dear! alas! bravo! hurra!
hark! hush! are all Interjections.

Examination on the Parts of Speech.—How many
Parts of Speech are there?—Repeat their names.—
Describe them.—Give examples of each.

The following short sentence contains all the
nine parts of speech:

1   3   2   4   5   6   8
John is a good boy; he learns well, and runs
7   9
to school: bravo!

CONCISE ILLUSTRATION OF THE PARTS OF SPEECH.

" A beautiful girl walks gracefully and modestly in the valley below."

In this sentence, which is a partial description of a single object and its phenomena,

A is the non-particularizing indicator [Indefinite Article].

Girl is the object [Noun].

Beautiful is one of her attributes or qualities [Adjective].

Walks is her motion [Verb].

Gracefully, modestly, are modifications of her motion [Adverbs].

And is a connective, and joins the Adverbs [Copulative Conjunction].

In the valley below is her accident of place, a prepositional phrase, containing *in* and *below* [two simple Prepositions].

The is the particularizing indicator [Definite Article].

Recapitulatory Exercises on the Parts of Speech, to which the teacher may add many others (orally) of similar construction:

A large stone rolls heavily and slowly towards the river.

That little boy stands uprightly and firmly near the edge of the precipice.

NOTE.—The pupil must go through the whole of the First Part again, before he begins with the Second. By so doing, his future progress will be much more rapid.

PART SECOND.

Lesson I.

ORTHOGRAPHY.—*Letters and Syllables.*

There are *twenty-six letters* used in the English language, and they are called the ENGLISH ALPHABET.

Spoken words are sounds which we make and utter with our throat, tongue, and mouth, by means of our breath ; and we use letters to stand for, or represent, those sounds. The twenty-six letters of the alphabet are of two kinds,—

Vowels and Consonants.

A Vowel is a sound which can be perfectly uttered by itself; as, *a, e, i, o, u.*

A Consonant is a sound which cannot be perfectly uttered without the help of a vowel; as *b, d, f, l, m, p, q.*

The are seven Vowels, namely:

a, e, i, o, u, w, y.

W is pronounced like *oo* ; *Y* pronounced like *e.*

There are nineteen Consonants, namely:

b, c, d, f, g, h, j, k, l, m, n, p, q, r, s, t, v, x, z.

NOTE.— *W* and *Y* are said to be *consonants* when they begin words or syllables, but *vowels* in every other situation. Upon a careful analysis of their powers and functions, we have no hesitation in declaring, that *W* and *Y* are INVARIABLY *vowels,* in EVERY *situation.*—For proofs and illustrations, see p. 26.

THE ENGLISH ALPHABET.

The following is a list of the Roman and the Italic Characters.

ROMAN.		ITALIC.		NAME.
Cap.	Small.	Cap.	Small.	
A	a	*A*	*a*	*ay*
B	b	*B*	*b*	*bee*
C	c	*C*	*c*	*see*
D	d	*D*	*d*	*dee*
E	e	*E*	*e*	*ce*
F	f	*F*	*f*	*ef*
G	g	*G*	*g*	*jee*
H	h	*H*	*h*	*aitch*
I	i	*I*	*i*	*i* or *eye*
J	j	*J*	*j*	*jay*
K	k	*K*	*k*	*kay*
L	l	*L*	*l*	*el*
M	m	*M*	*m*	*em*
N	n	*N*	*n*	*en*
O	o	*O*	*o*	*o*
P	p	*P*	*p*	*pee*
Q	q	*Q*	*q*	*cue*
R	r	*R*	*r*	*ar*
S	s	*S*	*s*	*ess*
T	t	*T*	*t*	*tee*
U	u	*U*	*u*	*u* or *you*
V	v	*V*	*v*	*vee*
W	w	*W*	*w*	*double u*
X	x	*X*	*x*	*cks*
Y	y	*Y*	*y*	*wy*
Z	z	*Z*	*z*	*zed*

Consonants are divided into Mutes and Semi-vowels.

Mutes

cannot be sounded *at all* without the aid of a vowel.

The Mutes are *b, p, t, d, k,* and *c* and *g hard.*

Semivowels

have an imperfect sound of themselves.

The Semivowels are *f, l, m, n, r, v, s, z, x,* and *c g* soft.

Liquids.

Four of the Semivowels are also called *Liquids,* from their easily uniting with other consonants, and flowing, as it were, into their sounds.

The Liquids are *l, m, n, r.*

Lesson II.

Diphthongs and Triphthongs.

A Diphthong is the union of two vowels pronounced by a single exertion of the voice; as,

ca in beat, *ou* in sound.

A Triphthong is the union of three vowels, pronounced by a single exertion of the voice; as,

eau in beau, *iew* in view, *ieu* in lieu.

A *Proper* Diphthong is that in which both the vowels are sounded; as,

oi in voice, *ou* in ounce.

An *Improper* Diphthong has only one of the vowels sounded; as,

ea in eagle, *oa* in boat.

A Syllable is a sound either simple or compounded, pronounced by a single impulse of the voice, and forming a word, or part of a word; as

a, an, ant, voice.

A word of one syllable is called a *Monosyllable ;* as,

man, great, strive.

A word of two syllables is called a *Dissyllable ;* as,

man-kind, gar-den, beau-ty.

A word of three syllables is called a *Trisyllable ;* as,

beau-ti-ful, in-dus-try.

A word of four or more syllables is called a *Polysyllable ;* as,

pre-ser-va-tion, in-di-vi-si-bi-li-ty.

Lesson III.

ETYMOLOGY.—*Parts of Speech.*

What is Speech?—Speech is talking; and talking is saying words that have some meaning. Every Speech is made up of words, and every word is a *Part of Speech.*

The English Language consists of about fifty thousand words, which are divided into nine different sorts or kinds.

All the people in the world amount to about eight hundred millions, but they have been divided and arranged into *five different families*, according to their country and color; namely :

1. The family of the *Blacks*— (Ethiopian).
2. The family of the *Browns*—(Malayan).
3. The family of the *Reds*— (American.)
4. The family of the *Yellows*—(Mongolian).
5. The family of the *Whites*— (European).

In the same manner the fifty thousand Words in the English Language have been divided into *nine different families*, according to their quality, or sort, or kind; namely :

1. The *Noun* family.
2. The *Adjective* family.
3. The *Article* family.
4. The *Pronoun* family.
5. The *Verb* family.
6. The *Adverb* family.
7. The *Preposition* family.
8. The *Conjunction* family.
And
9. The *Interjection* family.

Lesson IV.

NOUNS OR SUBSTANTIVES.

A Noun (which is also called a Substantive) is the name of any person, place, or thing ; such as man, Quebec, hat.

Nouns are of two kinds,—Proper Nouns and Common Nouns.

1. PROPER NOUNS.

Words which are used to point out particular persons, or particular places, are *Proper Nouns;* such as George, Mary, England, France, London, Canada, Thames, Seine, Danube.

2. COMMON NOUNS.

Words which are used for every person, or every place, or every thing of the same kind, are *Common Nouns ;* such as *man, town, city, village, horse, river, house, hammer, shoe.*

Words which mean a number of persons, or a number of animals, or a number of things, taken or seen together, are *Common Nouns ;* such as *army, crowd, people, herd, flock, congregation, audience, library, museum.* These are called Nouns of Multitude, or *Collective* Nouns.

The names of qualities, or states, or feelings, are Common Nouns ; such as *vice, gratitude, kindness, health, love, hatred, strength, light, darkness.* These are called *Abstract* Nouns.

Names of actions are Common Nouns ; such as *reading, writing, sleeping, walking.* These are called *Verbal* Nouns.

EXERCISES ON NOUNS.

The pupil must point-out the various kinds of Nouns in the following list :

Montreal,	horse,	moon,	regiment,
tree,	England,	star,	library,
nation,	stream,	Jupiter,	store,
lake,	house,	Mars,	forest,
France,	Dublin,	Saturn,	prairie,
dog,	garden,	planets,	patience,
mountain,	America,	girl,	industry,
Thames,	Spain,	road,	Eliza,
soldier,	woman,	goodness,	dictionary,
valley,	John,	wickedness,	sea.

Lesson V.

NUMBER,—*Singular and Plural.*

A Noun may mean one person, or object; or it may mean two, three, four, or more.

When it means only one, it is said to be *Singular;* when it means more than one, it is said to be *Plural.*

Thus you see and understand that Nouns have two Numbers,—the Singular and the Plural.

When we say a house, a tree, a chair, a table we speak in the *Singular* number.

When we say houses, trees, chairs, tables, we speak in the *Plural* Number.

RULES FOR FORMING THE PLURAL.

Rule 1.—Nouns are generally changed from the singular to the plural by adding an *s* to the singular: as,

book, books;	room, rooms;	coat, coats;
cow, cows;	stone, stones;	shoe, shoes;
street, streets;	ships, ships;	boy, boys;
hat, hats;	river, rivers;	girl, girls.

Rule 2.—But when the singular Nouns end in

s, st, sh, ch soft, z, x, or o,

they are changed into the plural by adding *es;* as,

Miss,	Misses;	fox,	foxes;
brush,	brushes;	box,	boxes;
church,	churches;	hero,	heroes;
match,	matches;	cargo,	cargoes;
lash,	lashes;	negro,	negroes.

Rule 3.—Many Nouns which end in *f* or *fe*, are made plural by changing the *f* or *fe* into *ves* : as,

loaf,	loaves ;		knife,	knives ;
leaf,	leaves ;		calf,	calves ;
half,	halves ;		shelf,	shelves ;
wife,	wives ;		wolf,	wolves ;
life,	lives ;		staff,	staves.

Rule 4.—Nouns which end in *y* in the singular, with no other vowel in the same syllable, change the *y* into *ies* in the plural : as

beau*ty*, beau*ties* ; fl*y*, fl*ies* ; du*ty*, du*ties*.

But the *y* is not changed when their is another vowel in the syllable : as

key, keys ; delay, delays.

Some Nouns are irregular in making their plurals ; such as,

man,	men ;		tooth,	teeth ;
woman,	women ;		goose,	geese ;
child,	children ;		mouse,	mice ;
foot,	feet ;		louse,	lice ;
ox,	oxen ;		penny,	pence.

Some Nouns, from the nature of the things which they express, are used only in the singular number ; such as wheat, pitch, gold, sloth, wisdom.

Some Nouns are only used in the plural number : such as clothes, bellows, snuffers, scissors, ashes, riches.

Some Nouns are the same in both numbers ; such as deer, sheep, swine, salmon, vermin.

EXERCISES ON NUMBER.

1. Of what number is

book,	toys,	foxes,	roses,	river,
trees,	home,	house,	churches,	scenes,
plant,	fancy,	prints,	glove,	stars,
shrub,	mosses,	spoon,	silk,	berries,
globes,	glasses,	bears,	skies,	peach ?
planets,	state,	lilies,	hill,	

2. Tell the plural of the following Nouns, and give the rule for forming it.

Thus, " Knife, plural knives. Rule—Nouns ending in *f* or *fe* form the plural by changing *f* or *fe* into *ves*."

fox,	loaf,	fish,	inch,	knife,
book,	wish,	sex,	sky,	echo,
leaf,	duty,	box,	bounty,	loss,
candle,	calf,	coach,	army,	cargo,
wife,	story,	branch,	rock,	hope,
church,	glass,	street,	stone,	flower,
table,	study,	potato,	house,	city,
peach,	sheaf,	booby,	wolf,	distress.

Lesson VI.

GENDER OF NOUNS.

Gender is the distinction or difference of Nouns in speaking of males and females.

Nouns which mean males, are of the masculine gender; as, man, bull, king.

Nouns which mean females, are of the feminine gender; as, woman, cow, queen.

All nouns which mean objects which are *neither* males nor females, are called neuter; as, house, tree, stone.

Thus, we have three genders,—

The *Masculine*, the *Feminine*, and the *Neuter*.

Nouns which mean *either* males or females, such as parent, child, cousin, friend, neighbour, and the like, are said to be of the *common* gender, that is, either masculine or feminine.

There are three ways of pointing-out the gender or sex :

1. By different words ; as,

Boy	Girl	King	Queen
Bridegroom	Bride	Lord	Lady
Brother	Sister	Husband	Wife
Cock	Hen	Ram	Ewe
Colt	Filly	Sir	Madam
Earl	Countess	Son	Daughter
Father	Mother	Uncle	Aunt
Gander	Goose	Widower	Widow
Gentleman	Lady	Wizard	Witch

2. By a different termination ; as,

Abbot	Abbess	Conductor	Conductress
Actor	Actress	Count	Countess
Author	Authoress	Peer	Peeress
Baron	Baroness	Poet	Poetess
Duke	Duchess	Priest	Priestess
Emperor	Empress	Prince	Princess
Executor	Executrix	Prior	Prioress
Giant	Giantess	Prophet	Prophetess
Governor	Governess	Protector	Protectress
Heir	Heiress	Shepherd	Shepherdess
Hero	Heroine	Songster	Songstress
Host	Hostess	Sultan	Sultana
Jew	Jewess	Tiger	Tigress
Lion	Lioness	Traitor	Traitress
Marquis	Marchioness	Tutor	Tutoress

3. By prefixing a Noun, an Adjective, **or a** Pronoun ; as,

Man-servant .... Maid-servant.
Cock-sparrow .... Hen-sparrow.
Male-child .... Female-child.
He-goat .... She-goat.

Lesson VII.

The Cases of Nouns.

When we use the word Case in grammar, it means state or situation, or position or relation.

A Noun may be, at different times, in different *states* or *situations*, or *positions* or *relations*, with regard to other Nouns in the same sentence.

For example, a Noun may be the name of a man who *strikes* a horse; or a Noun may be the name of a man who *has* a horse, or *possesses* a horse; or a Noun may be the name of a man whom a horse *kicks*. Here, you see, are three Cases.

In the first Case—John *strikes* the horse.

In the second Case—
{ John *possesses* a horse.
{ The horse is John's.
{ It is John's horse.

In the third Case—The horse *kicks John*.

When a Noun points-out to us a person or thing that *does* something, or *is* something, that Noun is always said to be in the *Nominative Case*. [Our English word Nominative is made from the Latin word *nomen*, which means a name.]

In the first case, where John *strikes* the horse, the word *John* is in the *Nominative Case*, because it is the name of a person who does something.

In the second case, where the horse is John's, or it is John's horse, the word *John's* is in the *Possessive Case*, because John possesses the horse.

In the third case, where the horse *kicks* John, John is neither the person who does anything, nor the person who possesses anything, but the *object* the horse kicks,—he is the *object* of the action of the horse : there the word *John* is in the *Objective Case*.

In English, Nouns have three Cases,—the Nominative, the Possessive, and the Objective.

The Nominative Case simply expresses the name of a thing, or the subject of the verb ; as, "The boy plays," "The girls learn."

The Possessive Case expresses the relation of property or possession, and has an apostrophe with the letter *s* coming after it ; as, "The scholar's duty," "My father's house."

When the plural ends in *s*, the other *s* is omitted, but the apostrophe is retained ; as, "On eagles' wings," "The drapers' company."

Sometimes also, when the singular terminates in *ss*, the apostrophic *s* is not added ; as, "For goodness' sake," "For righteousness' sake."

When a Noun in the possessive case ends in *ence*, the *s* is omitted, but the apostrophe is retained ; as, "For conscience' sake," "For convenience' sake."

The Objective Case expresses the object of an action or of a relation ; and generally follows a verb active, or a preposition : as, "John assists Charles," "They live in London."

English Nouns are declined in the following manner:

	Singular.	Plural.
Nominative Case,	A mother,	Mothers.
Possessive Case,	A mother's,	Mothers'.
Objective Case,	A mother,	Mothers.
Nominative Case,	The man,	The men.
Possessive Case,	The man's,	The men's.
Objective Case,	The man,	The men.

Lesson VIII.

ADJECTIVES.

An Adjective is a word added to a Noun to explain its quality or state; as, a *sharp* knife, a *high* mountain, a *heavy* weight.

When we compare two sharp knives together, we find that one cuts better than the other; we therefore say that it is *sharper* than the other.

When we compare two high mountains with each other, and we find that the top of·the one is several yards above the top of the other, we say that the one is *higher* than the other.

When we compare two heavy weights, and we find that one of them takes more strength to lift it than it does to lift the other, we say the one is *heavier* than the other.

When we compare three sharp knives, we find that one has its sharpness in the greatest degree; we therefore say it is the *sharpest.*

So, when we compare three mountains, we say of the one whose top reaches farthest up, that it is the *highest.*

So also, when we compare three heavy weights, we say of the one which is most difficult to be lifted, that it is the *heaviest.*

So you see that Adjectives have THREE DE-GREES OF COMPARISON : these degrees are called

The *Positive,* the *Comparative,* and the *Superlative.*

The Positive state simply expresses or tells the quality of an object, without any increase or diminution ; as,

> *good — wise — great.* ·

The Comparative increases or lessens the Positive in its degree ; as

> *wise — wis:r — less wise.*

The Superlative increases or lessens the Positive to the highest or to the lowest degree ; as,

> *wisest — greatest — least wise.*

The simple word, or Positive, becomes the Comparative by adding *r* or *er,* and it becomes the Superlative by adding *st* or *est,* to the end of it ; as,

> *wise — wiser — wisest.*
> *great — greater — greatest.*

And the Adverbs *more* and *most,* placed before the Adjective, have the same effect ; as,

> *wise — more wise — most wise.*

Words of one syllable are nearly all compared by *er* and *est;* as,

mild,	milder,	mildest,
bright,	brighter,	brightest,
fine,	finer,	finest.

But words of two or more syllables are compared by placing the Adverbs *more* and *most* before them ; as,

careful, *more* careful, *most* careful.
beautiful, *more* beautiful, *most* beautiful.

Some Adjectives that are very much used, have different words for the Comparative and the Superlative ; as,

good,	better,	best.
bad, evil, ill,	worse,	worst.
little,	less,	least.
much or many,	more,	most.

Lesson IX.

PRONOUNS.

A Pronoun is a word used instead of a Noun, to avoid the too-frequent repetition of the same word ; as, John is happy, *he* is benevolent, *he* is useful.

There are three kinds of Pronouns,—

Personal Pronouns.
Relative Pronouns.
Adjective Pronouns.

1. Personal Pronouns.

The Personal Pronouns are used instead of mentioning the names of the persons.

When we speak of ourselves or of others, we very seldom mention our names ; but we say, *I* shall go, *thou* wilt return, *he* is here, *she* was diligent ; and if the object be an animal, or a tree, we say, *it* runs, or *it* grows.

Thus, we have five Personal Pronouns ; namely, *I, thou, he, she, it ;* with their Plurals, *we, ye* or *you, they.*

Personal Pronouns are either Singular or Plural.

I is the first person	
Thou is the second person	Singular.
He, she, or *it* is the third person	
We is the first person	
Ye or *you* is the second person	Plural.
They is the third person	

The Three Persons.

The person *speaking* is the First Person.
The person *spoken* TO is the second.
The person or thing *spoken* OF is the third.

For instance,—

> *I* can assure *you* that *he* is coming.

I is the first person, being the *speaker ;*
You is the second person, being *spoken* TO ;
He is the third person, being *spoken* OF.

To Personal Pronouns belong Person, Gender, Number, and Case, all of which you will easily understand by learning the following table :

PLAN OF THE PERSONAL PRONOUNS,

Showing their Persons, Genders, Numbers, and Cases.

	Case.	Singular.	Plural.
First Person	Nom......I,.........We.		
	Poss.......Mine, ...Ours.		
	Obj. ......Me,.......Us.		
Second Person	Nom......Thou, ...Ye or you.		
	Poss.......Thine,.....Yours.		
	Obj. ......Thee,......You.		
Third Person Masculine	Nom......He, ...They.		
	Poss.......His,.......Theirs.		
	Obj. ......Him,......Them.		
Third Person Feminine	Nom......She, ...They.		
	Poss.......Hers,......Theirs.		
	Obj. ......Her, ...Them.		
Third Person Neuter	Nom......It, ...They.		
	Poss.......Its, ...Theirs.		
	Obj. ......It, ...Them.		

When Nouns or Pronouns are placed in order, so as to show all their Persons, Genders, Numbers, and Cases, the plan or table is called a *Declension;* and when the pupil repeats it in order, from beginning to end, he *declines* it.

Lesson X.

The word *antecedent* is a word very much used in Grammar,—its exact meaning is *going before.* It is always used to point-out some word or phrase *going before* some other word or phrase.

2. RELATIVE PRONOUNS.

Relative Pronouns are such as relate to some word or phrase *going before*, which is therefore called the *antecedent.* The relative Pronouns are

who, which, and *that;*

as, the man is happy *who* lives virtuously.
What is a kind of compound relative, including both the antecelent and the relative, and mostly means *that which;* as,

This is *what* I wanted,—

that is to say, *the thing which* I wanted.

Who is used chiefly of persons ;
Which is used of animals and other things : as,

He is a friend *who* is faithful in adversity ;
The bird *which* sung so sweetly is flown ;
This is the tree *which* produces no fruit.

That is often used to prevent the too-frequent repetition of *who* and *which.* It is applied to both persons and things : as,

He that acts wisely deserves praise ;
Modesty is a *quality that* adorns a woman.

Who is both Singular and Plural, and is thus declined :

Nominative......*Who.*
Possessive.......*Whose.*
Objective ....*Whom.*

Who, which, what, when used to ask questions, are called *Interrogative Pronouns;* as,

Who is he ?
Which is the book ?
What are you doing ?

Lesson XI.

3. ADJECTIVE PRONOUNS.

Adjective Pronouns are of a mixed nature; they have the qualities or properties of both Pronouns and Adjectives.

Adjective Pronouns are of four sorts; namely,
1. Possessive.　　3. Demonstrative.
2. Distributive.　　4. Indefinite.

1. POSSESSIVE PRONOUNS

Are those which relate to possession or property. There are nine of them:

1. My.　　4. Her.　　7. Your.
2. Thy.　　5. Its.　　8. Their.
3. His.　　6. Our.　　9. Own.

EXAMPLES.

My lesson is finished.　We own *our* faults.
Thy book is torn.　*Your* situation is good.
He loves *his* studies.　I admire *their* wisdom.
She performs *her* duty.　This book is *my own*.
Virtue is *its* own reward. This is *our own* farm.

2. DISTRIBUTIVE PRONOUNS

Are those which point-out the persons or things that make-up a number, when taken separately or singly. They are,

each, every, either, neither.

EXAMPLES.

Each of the voters received a bribe.
Every man must account for himself.
I have not seen *either* of them.

Either relates to two persons or things taken separately, and means the one or the other. To say " *either* of the three " is therefore improper.

Neither means *not either ;* that is, not one nor the other : for example,

Neither of my friends was there.

To say " *neither* of the three " is therefore improper.

3. Demonstrative Pronouns

Are those which point-out exactly the persons or things to which they relate : they are,

Singular.	Plural.
This,	These.
That,	Those.

This means the nearest person or thing, and *that* means the most distant ; as, *This* man is more intelligent than *that.*

This means the latter or last mentioned ; *That* means the former or first mentioned : as, Both wealth and poverty are temptations ; *that* is likely to make us proud, *this* is likely to make us discontented.

Lesson XII.

4. Indefinite Pronouns

Are those which express their meaning in a very general manner. The principal are,

one,	some,	other,
none,	any,	another,
all,	both,	whoever,
whole,	such,	whatever.

One, meaning a particular number (a unit), is a Numeral Adjective ; as, " *One* man is sufficient, " " I have only *one* dollar." In these two cases the word *one* is a Numeral Adjective.

But when the word *one* does not mean any particular individual, it is an Indefinite Pronoun ; for example,

One man's interest is not preferred to another's.

One's interest is as good as another's.

One is as good as another.

He took the old bird, and left the young *ones*.

One might say.

In all these cases the word *one* is an Indefinite Pronoun.

The words *other* and *another*, may, in like manner, be used both as Adjectives and as Indefinite Pronouns.

ILLUSTRATIONS.

Some of them are wise and good.

A few of them were idle ; the *others* were industrious.

There is not *any* that is unexceptionable.

One ought to know *one's* mind.

They were *all* present.

Some are happy, while *others* are miserable.

None is so deaf as he who will not hear.

Although the word *none* is made-up of *no* and *one*, and means *no one*, which is Singular, yet it is frequently used in the Plural : as,

None of the pupils *have* left the school ;

None of the books *are* well bound.

VERBS.

[*Read Lesson VIII., Part I., page* 17.]

A Verb is a word which signifies to be, to do, or to suffer (or be done to).

| *To Be,* | *To Do,* | *To Be done to,* |
| I am. | I rule. | I am ruled. |

Thus you see Verbs are of three kinds,—

ACTIVE, PASSIVE, NEUTER.

When a Verb means TO DO *something*, or *to act upon*, it is called an ACT*I*VE *Verb.*

When a Verb means TO SUFFER *something*, or *to be acted upon*, it is called a PASSIVE *Verb.*

When a Verb means TO BE *something*, it is called a NEUTER *Verb.*

When a Verb means an action which does not pass from the person who performs the action to any other object, it is also called a NEUTER *Verb;* as I *ride*, I *walk*, I *swim.*

A *Verb Active* expresses an action, and necessarily implies an agent or actor, and an object acted upon : as,

To love ; I love Penelopé.

A *Verb Passive* expresses a *passion*, a *suffering*, or the *receiving of an action;* and it necessarily implies an object acted upon, and an agent by which it is acted upon : as,

To be loved ; Penelopé is loved by me.

A *Verb Neuter* expresses neither action nor passion, but *being*, or *a state of being :* as,

I am ; I sleep ; I sit.

To Verbs belong *Number* and *Person.*

Verbs have two Numbers, the Singular and the Plural ; as,

Singular—He runs.   Plural—They run, &c.

In each Number there are three Persons ; as,

	Singular.	*Plural.*
First Person	—I love.	We love.
Second Person	—Thou lovest.	You love.
Third Person	—He loves.	They love.

To Verbs belong *Moods* and *Participles.*

Mood or Mode is a particular form of the Verb, showing the manner in which the *Being,* or the *Doing,* or the *Being Done to,* is represented.

There are five Moods of Verbs,—

1. Indicative.
2. Imperative.
3. Potential.
4. Subjunctive.
5. Infinitive.

1. The *Indicative Mood* simply indicates or declares a thing: as,

He loves ; he is loved.

Or it asks a question : as,

Does he love ?   Is he loved ?

2. The *Imperative Mood* is used for command- ing, exhorting, entreating, or permitting : as,

Depart thou   (*commanding*).
Mind you   (*exhorting*).
Let us stay   (*entreating*).
Go in peace   (*permitting*).

3. The *Potential Mood* expresses possibility, liberty, power, will, or obligation, as,

It may rain	(*possibility*).
He may go or stay	(*liberty*).
I can ride	(*power*).
He would walk	(*will*).
They should learn	(*obligation*).

4. The *Subjunctive Mood* represents a thing under a condition, motive, wish, supposition, &c., and is preceded by a Conjunction, expressed or understood, and attended by another Verb: as,

I will respect him, *though* he chide me;
Were he good, he would be happy,—

that is, *if* he were good.

5. The *Infinitive Mood* expresses an act or state in a general and unlimited manner, without any distinction of number or person : as,

To act; to speak ; to be feared.

Participles.

The Participle is a certain form of the Verb, and derives its name from its possessing, not only the properties of a Verb, but also those of an Adjective: as,

I am desirous of *knowing* him ;
Admired and *applauded*, he became vain ;
Having finished his work, he submitted it.

There are three Participles,—the Present or Active, the Perfect or Passive, and the Compound Perfect; as,

Present.	Perfect.	Compound Perfect.
Loving,	Loved,	Having loved.
Walking,	Walked,	Having walked.

The Tenses, or *Times.*

The plain and obvious distinctions of time are only three ; namely, *Present, Past,* and *Future.*

But in order to enable us to mark it more exactly, it is made to consist of *six variations,*—

1. The Present.
2. The Imperfect Past.
3. The Perfect Past.
4. The Pluperfect Past.
5. The First Future.
6. The Second Future.

1. The *Present Tense* represents an action, or event, as passing at the time in which it is mentioned: as,

I rule ; I am ruled ; I think ; I fear.

The *Imperfect Tense* represents an action or event, either as past and finished, or as remaining unfinished, at a certain time past: as,

I *loved her* for her modesty and virtue ;
They *were travelling* post when he met them.

The *Perfect Tense* not only refers to what is past, but also conveys an allusion to the present time: as,

I *have finished* my letter ;
I *have seen* the person that was recommended.

The *Pluperfect Tense* represents a thing, not only as past, but also as prior to some other point of time mentioned in the sentence ; as,

I *had finished* my letter before he arrived.

The *First Future Tense* represents the action, or state, as yet to come, either with or without respect to the precise time : as,

The sun *will rise* to-morrow ;
I *shall see* them again.

The *Second Future Tense* intimates that the action will be fully accomplished at or before the time of another future action or event: as,

I *shall have dined* at one o'clock;
He *will have finished* his exercises before his father comes.

There are five classes of Verbs, namely:

1. Auxiliary Verbs.
2. Regular Verbs.
3. Irregular Verbs.

4. Defective Verbs.
5. Impersonal Verbs

What is a Conjugation?

The Conjugation of a Verb is the regular and correct arrangement of all its Moods, Tenses, Persons, and Numbers.

To *conjugate* a Verb is to say it, or repeat it, in all its Moods, Tenses, Persons, and Numbers.

AUXILIARY VERBS.

Auxiliary or Helping Verbs are those by the help of which the English Verbs are conjugated.

May,
Can,
Must,

Might,
Could,
Would,

Should,
and
Shall,

are always Auxiliaries.

Do, Be, Have, *and* Will,

are sometimes Auxiliaries, and sometimes principal Verbs.

The Auxiliary and Active Verb *To Have* is conjugated in the following manner:

4

Indicative Mood.

PRESENT TENSE.

Singular.	Plural.
1. *Pers.* I have.	1. We have.
2. *Pers.* Thou hast.	2. Ye *or* you have.
3. *Pers.* He, she, *or* it hath or has.	3. They have.

IMPERFECT TENSE.

Singular.	Plural.
1. I had.	1. We had.
2. Thou hadst.	2. Ye *or* you had.
3. He, &c. had.	3. They had.

FIRST FUTURE TENSE.

Singular.	Plural.
1. I shall *or* will have,	1. We shall *or* will have.
2. Thou shalt *or* wilt have.	2. Ye *or* you shall *or* will have.
3. He shall *or* will have.	3. They shall *or* will have.

PERFECT TENSE.

Singular.	Plural.
1. I have had.	1. We have had.
2. Thou hast had.]	2. Ye *or* you have had.
8. He has had.	3. They have had.

PLUPERFECT TENSE.

Singular.	Plural.
1. I had had.	1. We had had.
2. Thou hadst had.	2. Ye *or* you had had.
3. He had had.	3. They had had.

SECOND FUTURE TENSE.

Singular.	Plural.
1. I shall have had.	1. We shall have had.
2. Thou wilt have had.	2. Ye *or* you will have had.
3. He will have had.	3. They will have had.

Imperative Mood.

USED IN THE SECOND PERSON ONLY.

Singular.	Singular *or* Plural.
Have, *or* have thou, *or* do thou have.	Let me have.
	Let him have.
Plural.	Let us have.
Have, *or* have you, *or* do you have.	Let them have.

Potential Mood.

PRESENT TENSE.

Singular.	Plural.
1. I may *or* can have.	1. We may *or* can have.
2. Thou mayst *or* can have.	2. Ye *or* you may *or* can have.
3. He may *or* can have.	3. They may *or* can have.

IMPERFECT TENSE.

Singular.	Plural.
1. I might, could, would, *or* should have.	1. We might, could, would, *or* should have.
2. Thou mightst, couldst, wouldst *or* shouldst have.	2. Ye *or* you might, could, would, *or* should have.
3. He might, could, would, *or* should have.	3. They might, could, would, *or* should have.

PERFECT TENSE.

Singular.	Plural.
1. I may *or* can have had.	1. We may *or* can have had.
2. Thou mayst *or* canst have had.	2. Ye *or* you may *or* can have had.
3. He may *or* can have had.	3. They may *or* can have had.

PLUPERFECT TENSE.

Singular.	Plural.
1. I might, could, would, *or* should have had.	1. We might, could, would, *or* should have had.
2. Thou mightst, couldst, wouldst *or* shouldst have had.	2. Ye *or* you might, could, would, *or* should have had.
3. He might, could, would, *or* should have had.	3. They might, could, would, *or* should have had.

Subjunctive Mood.

PRESENT TENSE.

Singular.	Plural.
1. If I have.	1. If we have.
2. If thou have.	2. If ye *or* you have.
3. If he have.	3. If they have.

NOTE.—The remaining Tenses of the Subjunctive Mood are similar to the correspondent Tenses in the Indicative Mood.

Infinitive Mood.

PRESENT—To have. PERFECT—To have had.

Participles.

PRESENT OR ACTIVE—Having. PERFECT—Had.

COMPOUND PERFECT—Having had.

The Auxiliary and Neuter Verb *To Be* is conjugated as follows:

Indicative Mood.

PRESENT TENSE.

Singular.	*Plural.*
1. I am.	1. We are.
2. Thou art.	2. Ye *or* you are.
3. He, she, *or* it, is.	3. They are.

IMPERFECT TENSE.

Singular.	*Plural.*
1. I was.	1. We were.
2. Thou wast.	2. Ye *or* you were.
3. He was.	3. They were.

FIRST FUTURE TENSE.

Singular.	*Plural.*
1. I shall *or* will be.	1. We shall *or* will be.
2. Thou shalt *or* wilt be.	2. Ye *or* you shall *or* will **be.**
3. He shall *or* will be.	3. They shall *or* will be.

PERFECT TENSE.

Singular.	*Plural.*
1. I have been.	1. We have been.
2. Thou hast been.	2. Ye *or* you have been.
3. He has *or* hath been.	3. They have been.

PLUPERFECT TENSE.

Singular.	*Plural.*
1. I had been.	1. We had been.
2. Thou hadst been.	2. Ye *or* you had been.
3. He had been.	3. They had been.

SECOND FUTURE TENSE.

Singular.	*Plural.*
1. I shall have been.	1. We shall have been.
2. Thou wilt have been.	2. Ye *or* you will have **been.**
3. He will have been.	3. They will have been.

Imperative Mood.

USED IN THE SECOND PERSON ONLY.

Singular.	*Singular or Plural,*
Be, *or* be thou, *or* do thou be.	Let me be.
Plural.	Let him be.
Be *or* be you, *or* do ye be.	Let us be.
	Let them be.

Potential Mood.

PRESENT TENSE.

Singular.	*Plural.*
1. I may *or* can be.	1. We may *or* can be.
2. Thou mayst *or* canst be.	2. Ye *or* you may *or* can be.
3. He may *or* can be.	3. They may *or* can be.

IMPERFECT TENSE.

Singular.	*Plural.*
1. I might, could, would, *or* should be.	1. We might, could, would, *or* should be.
2. Thou mightst, couldst, wouldst, *or* shouldst be.	2. Ye *or* you might, could, would, *or* should be.
3. He might, could, would, *or* should be.	3. They might, could, would, *or* should be.

PERFECT TENSE.

Singular.	*Plural.*
1. I may *or* can have been.	1. We may *or* can have been.
2. Thou mayst *or* canst have been.	2. Ye *or* you may *or* can have been.
3. He may *or* can have been.	3. They may *or* can have been.

PLUPERFECT TENSE.

Singular.	*Plural.*
1. I might, could, would, *or* should have been.	1. We might, could, would, *or* should have been.
2. Thou mightst, couldst, wouldst, *or* shouldst have been.	2. Ye *or* you might, could, would *or* should have been.
3. He might, could, would, *or* should have been.	3. They might, could, would, *or* should have been.

Subjunctive Mood.

PRESENT TENSE.

Singular.	*Plural.*
1. If I be.	1. If we be.
2. If thou be.	2. If ye *or* you be.
3. If he be.	3. If they be.

IMPERFECT TENSE.

Singular.	*Plural.*
1. If I were.	1. If we were.
2. If thou wert.	2. If ye *or* you were.
3. If he were.	3. If they were.

Infinitive Mood.

Present Tense—To be. | *Perfect*—To have been.

Participles.

Present—Being. | *Perfect*—Been.

Compound Perfect—Having been.

The pupil will see that the Auxiliary Verbs *To Have* and *To Be* could not be conjugated through all the Moods and Tenses without the help of *other* Auxiliary Verbs ; namely, *may, can, will, shall,* and their variations.

The Auxiliary Verbs are very short, and very simple; they are chiefly useful in helping us to conjugate the principal Verbs.

The following are the Auxiliary Verbs, in their simple state :

1. To Have.

PRESENT TENSE.

Singular.	*Plural.*
1. I have.	1. We have.
2. Thou hast.	2. You have.
3. He has or hath.	3. They have.

IMPERFECT TENSE.

Singular.	*Plural.*
1. I had.	1. We had.
2. Thou hadst.	2. You had.
3. He had.	3. They had.

PERFECT TENSE.

Singular.	*Plural.*
1. I have had.	1. We have had.
2. Thou hast had.	2. You have had.
3. He has had.	3. They have had.

PLUPERFECT TENSE.

Singular.	*Plural.*
1. I had had.	1. We had had.
2. Thou hadst had.	2. You had had.
3. He had had.	3. They had had.

Participles.

Present—Having. | *Perfect*—Had.

2. To Be.

PRESENT TENSE.

Singular.	*Plural.*
1. I am.	1. We are.
2. Thou art.	2. You are.
3. He is.	3. They are.

IMPERFECT TENSE.

Singular.	Plural.
1. I was.	1. We were.
2. Thou wast.	2. You were.
3. He was.	3. They were.

Participles.

Present—Being. | *Perfect*—Been.

3. Shall.

PRESENT TENSE.

Singular.	Plural.
1. I shall.	1. We shall.
2. Thou shalt.	2. You shall.
3. He shall.	3. They shall.

IMPERFECT TENSE.

Singular.	Plural.
1. I should.	1. We should.
2. Thou shouldst.	2. You should.
3. He should.	3. They should.

4. Will.

PRESENT TENSE.

Singular.	Plural.
1. I will.	1. We will.
2. Thou wilt.	2. You will.
3. He will.	3. They will.

IMPERFECT TENSE.

Singular.	Plural.
1. I would.	1. We would.
2. Thou wouldst.	2. You would.
3. He would.	3. They would.

5. May.

PRESENT TENSE.

Singular.	Plural.
1. I may.	1. We may.
2. Thou mayst.	2. You may.
3. He may.	3. They may.

IMPERFECT TENSE.

Singular.	Plural.
1. I might.	1. We might.
2. Thou mightest.	2. You might.
3. He might.	3. They might.

6. Can.

PRESENT TENSE.

Singular.	*Plural.*
1. I can.	1. We can.
2. Thou canst.	2. You can.
3. He can.	3. They can.

IMPERFECT TENSE.

Singular.	*Plural.*
1. I could.	1. We could.
2. Thou couldst.	2. You could.
3. He could.	3. They could.

7. To Do.

PRESENT TENSE.

Singular.	*Plural.*
1. I do.	1. We do.
2. Thou dost.	2. You do.
3. He does.	3. They do.

IMPERFECT TENSE.

Singular.	*Plural.*
1. I did.	1. We did.
2. Thou didst.	2. You did.
3. He did.	3. They did.

8. LET, has no change.   9. MUST, has no change.

The Verbs *Have*, *Be*, *Will*, and *Do*, when they are not used with a principal Verb, are not Auxiliaries, but principal Verbs : as,

We *have* enough ;	He *wills* it to be so ;
I *am* grateful ;	They *do* as they please.

In these cases, they also have their Auxiliaries : as,

I sh*all have* enough ;	They *will be* grateful.

The peculiar force and meaning of the several Auxiliaries will appear from the following illustrations :

Do and *Did.*

Do and *Did* give greater strength and positiveness to the action, or the term of it : as,

I *do* speak truth ; I *did* respect him.
Here am I, for thou *didst* call me.

They are of great use in negative sentences : as,

Do not fear ; I *did not* write.

They sometimes also supply the place of another verb, and make the repetition of it, in the same, or a subsequent sentence, unnecessary ; as,

You attend-not to your duties as he *does* (that is, as he attends, &c.).
I shall come if I can ; but if I *do not*, please to excuse me (that is, if I come not).

Shall and *Will.*

Will, in the first person, singular and plural, expresses resolution and promising ; as,

I *will* reward the good, and *will* punish the wicked.
We *will* remember benefits, and be grateful.

In the second and third Persons, it only foretels ; as,

Thou *wilt*, or he *will*, repent of that folly. You, or they, *will* have a pleasant walk.

Shall, on the contrary, in the first person simply foretels ; in the second and third persons, it promises, or commands, or threatens ; as,

I *shall* go abroad. We *shall* dine at home.
Thou *shalt*, or you *shall*, inherit the land,
They *shall* account for their misconduct.

These observations upon the meaning of the verbs *Will* and *Shall*, must be understood of assertions, or explicative sentences; for when the sentence is interrogative, just the reverse, for the most part, takes place. Thus—

I *shall* go, you *will* go, express event only ; but

Will you go ? *will* they do that ? express intention.

Shall I go ? refers to the will of another.   He *shall* go, and *shall* he go ? both imply will; expressing or referring to a command.

When the Verb is put in the subjunctive mood, the meaning of these Auxiliaries likewise undergoes some alteration ; as the learner will readily perceive by a few examples :

He *shall* proceed.	You *shall* consent.
If he *shall* proceed.	If you *shall* consent.

These Auxiliaries are sometimes introduced in the Indicative and Subjunctive Moods, to convey the same meaning of the Auxiliary ; as,

He *will* not return.	He *shall* not return.
If he *shall* not return.	If he *will* not return.

Would and *Should*.

Would primarily denotes inclination of will, and *should* expresses obligation ; as

I *would* like to live in France,
But I *should* live in Canada.

Both, however, vary their import, and are often used to express simple event.

May and *Might*.

May and *Might* express the possibility or liberty of doing a thing ; as

It *may* rain.   I *may* write or read.   She *might* have improved more than she has.

Can and Could.

Can and *Could* express the power of doing a thing ; as,

He *can* write much better than he *could* last year.

Let.

Let not only expresses permission, but entreating, exhorting, commanding ; as,

Let us know the truth.
Let me die the death of the righteous.
Let not thy heart be too much elated.
Let thy inclinations submit to thy duty.

Must.

Must is sometimes called-in for a helper, and expresses necessity : as,

We *must* speak the truth, whenever we do speak ; and we must not prevaricate.

The Conjugation of Regular Verbs.

ACTIVE.

Verbs Active are called Regular when they form the Imperfect Tense of the Indicative Mood, and the Perfect Participle, by adding to the Verb ED ; or D only, when the Verb ends in E : as,

Present.	Imperfect.	Perfect Participle.
I favour,	I favored,	Favored.
I love,	I loved,	Loved.

A Regular Active Verb is conjugated in the following manner,—example, *To love.*

Indicative Mood.

PRESENT TENSE.

Singular.	*Plural.*
1 *Person*, I Love.	1. We love.
2 *Person*, Thou lovest.	2. You love.
3 *Person*, He, she, *or* it loves *or* loveth.	3. They love.

IMPERFECT PAST TENSE.

Singular.	*Plural.*
1. I loved.	1. We loved.
2. Thou lovedst.	2. You loved.
3. He loved.	3. They loved.

FIRST FUTURE TENSE.

Singular.	*Plural.*
1. I shall *or* will love.	1. We shall *or* will love.
2. Thou shalt *or* wilt love.	2. You shall *or* will love.
3. He shall *or* will love.	3. They shall *or* will love.

PERFECT PAST TENSE.

Singular.	*Plural.*
1. I have loved.	1. We have loved.
2. Thou hast loved.	2. You have loved.
3. He has loved.	3. They have loved.

PLUPERFECT PAST TENSE.

Singular.	*Plural.*
1. I had loved.	1. We had loved.
2. Thou hadst loved.	2. You had loved.
3. He had loved.	3. They had loved.

SECOND FUTURE TENSE.

Singular.	*Plural.*
1. I shall *or* will have loved.	1. We shall *or* will have loved.
2. Thou shalt *or* wilt have loved	2. You shall *or* will have loved.
3. He shall *or* will have loved.	3. They shall *or* will have loved.

Imperative Mood.

USED IN THE SECOND PERSON ONLY.

Singular.	*Singular or Plural.*
Love, *or* love thou, *or* do thou love.	Let me love.
	Let him love.
Plural.	Let us love.
Love, *or* love you, *or* do you love.	Let them love.

Potential Mood.

PRESENT TENSE.

Singular.	*Plural.*
1. I may *or* can love.	1. We may *or* can love.
2. Thou mayst *or* canst love.	2. You may *or* can love.
3. He may *or* can love.	3. They may *or* can love.

IMPERFECT PAST TENSE.

Singular.	*Plural.*
1. I might, could, would, *or* should love.	1. We might, could, would, *or* should love.
2. Thou mightst, couldst, wouldst, *or* shouldst love.	2. You might, could, would, *or* should love.
3. He might, could, would, *or* should love.	3. They might, could, would, *or* should love.

PERFECT PAST TENSE.

Singular.	*Plural.*
1. I may *or* can have loved.	1. We may *or* can have loved.
2. Thou mayst *or* canst have loved.	2. You may *or* can have loved.
3. He may *or* can have loved.	3. They may *or* can have loved.

PLUPERFECT PAST TENSE.

Singular.	*Plural.*
1. I might, could, would, *or* should have loved.	1. We might, could, would, *or* should have loved.
2. Thou mightst, couldst, wouldst, *or* shouldst have loved.	2. You might, could, would, *or* should have loved.
3. He might, could, would, *or* should have loved.	3. They might, could, would, *or* should have loved.

Subjunctive Mood.

PRESENT TENSE.

Singular.	*Plural.*
1. If I love.	1. If we love.
2. If thou love.	2. If you love.
3. If he love.	3. If they love.

NOTE.—The remaining Tenses of this Mood are similar to the correspondent Tenses of the Indicative Mood.

Infinitive Mood.

PRESENT—To love. | PERFECT—To have loved.

Participles.

PRESENT—Loving. | PERFECT—Loved.

COMPOUND PERFECT—Having loved.

PASSIVE VERBS.

A Passive Verb is conjugated by adding the Perfect Participle to the Auxiliary *To Be*, through all its changes of number, person, mood, and tense, in the following manner:

TO BE LOVED.
Indicative Mood.

PRESENT TENSE.

Singular.	*Plural.*
1. I am loved.	1. We are loved.
2. Thou art loved.	2. Ye *or* you are loved.
3. He is loved.	3. They are loved.

IMPERFECT TENSE.

Singular.	*Plural.*
1. I was loved.	1. We were loved.
2. Thou wast loved.	2. Ye *or* you were loved.
3. He was loved.	3. They were loved.

FIRST FUTURE TENSE.

Singular.	*Plural.*
1. I shall *or* will be loved.	1. We shall *or* will be loved.
2. Thou shalt *or* wilt be loved.	2. Ye *or* you shall *or* will be loved.
3. He shall *or* will be loved.	3. They shall *or* will be loved.

PERFECT TENSE.

Singular.	*Plural.*
1. I have been loved.	1. We have been loved.
2. Thou hast been loved.	2. Ye *or* you have been loved.
3. He has *or* hath been loved.	3. They have been loved.

PLUPERFECT TENSE.

Singular.	*Plural.*
1. I had been loved.	1. We had been loved.
2. Thou hadst been loved.	2. Ye *or* you had been loved.
3. He had been loved.	3. They had been loved.

SECOND FUTURE TENSE.

Singular.	*Plural.*
1. I shall have been loved.	1. We shall have been loved.
2. Thou wilt have been loved.	2. Ye *or* you will have been loved.
3. He will have been loved.	3. They will have been loved.

Imperative Mood.

USED IN THE SECOND PERSON ONLY.

Singular.	*Singular or Plural.*
Be loved, *or* be thou loved, *or* do thou be loved.	Let me be loved.
Plural.	Let him be loved.
Be loved, *or* be you loved, *or* do you be loved.	Let us be loved.
	Let them be loved.

Potential Mood.

PRESENT TENSE.

Singular.	*Plural.*
1. I may *or* can be loved.	1. We may *or* can be loved.
2. Thou mayst *or* canst be loved.	2. Ye *or* you may *or* can be loved.
3. He may *or* can be loved.	3. They may *or* can be loved.

IMPERFECT TENSE.

Singular.	*Plural.*
1. I might, could, would, *or* should be loved.	1. We might, could, would, *or* should be loved.
2. Thou mightst, couldst, wouldst, *or* shouldst be loved.	2. Ye *or* you might, could, would, *or* should be loved.
3. He might, could, would, *or* should be loved.	3. They might, could, would, *or* should be loved.

PERFECT TENSE.

Singular.	*Plural.*
1. I may *or* can have been loved.	1. We may *or* can have been loved.
2. Thou mayst *or* canst have been loved.	2. Ye *or* you may *or* can have been loved.
3. He may *or* can have been loved.	3. They may *or* can have been loved.

PLUPERFECT TENSE.

Singular.	*Plural.*
1. I might, could, would, *or* should have been loved.	1. We might, could, would, *or* should have been loved.
2. Thou mightst, couldst, wouldst, *or* shouldst have been loved.	2. Ye *or* you might, could, would, *or* should have been loved.
3. He might, could, would, *or* should have been loved.	3. They might, could, would, *or* should have been loved.

Subjunctive Mood.

PRESENT TENSE.

Singular.	*Plural.*
1. If I be loved.	1. If we be loved.
2. If thou be loved.	2. If ye *or* you be loved.
3. If he be loved.	3. If they be loved.

IMPERFECT TENSE.

Singular.	*Plural.*
1. If I were loved.	1. If we were loved.
2. If thou were loved.	2. If ye *or* you were loved.
3. If he were loved.	3. If they were loved.

NOTE.—The remaining Tenses of this Mood are all similar to the correspondent Tenses of the Indicative Mood.

Infinitive Mood.

Present Tense—To be loved. | *Perfect*—To have been loved.

Participles.

PRESENT—Being loved. | PERFECT OR PASSIVE—Loved.
COMPOUND PERFECT—Having been loved.

Verbs Passive are called regular when they form their perfect participle by the addition of *d* or *ed* to the verb; as, from the Verb "To love," is formed the passive, "I am loved, I was loved, I shall be loved," &c.

OBSERVATIONS.

When an Auxiliary is joined to the Participle of the principal Verb, the Auxiliary goes through all the variations of person and number, and the Participle itself continues invariably the same.

When there are two or more Auxiliaries joined to the Participle, the first of them only is varied according to person and number.

The Auxiliary *must* admits of no variations.

NEUTER VERBS.

The Neuter Verb is conjugated like the Active; but as it partakes somewhat of the Passive, it admits, in many instances, of the passive form, retaining still the neuter signification; as, "I am arrived," "I was gone," "I am grown." The Auxiliary Verb *Am*, *Was*, in this case, precisely defines the time of the action or event, but does not change the nature of it; the passive form still expressing, not properly a passion, but only a state or condition of being.

IRREGULAR VERBS.

Regular Verbs form their Past Tense and their Past Participle, by adding *d* or *ed* to the Present; as,

I love, I loved, I have loved.

Irregular Verbs are those which *do not* form the Past Tense and the Past Participle by adding *d* or *ed* to the Present; as,

Present.	Past.	Past Part.
I begin,	I began,	begun.
I know,	I knew,	known.

IRREGULAR VERBS are of various sorts.

1. Such as have the present and past tenses, and the past participle, the same; as,

Present.	Past.	Past Part.
Cost,	cost,	cost
Put,	put,	put.

2. Such as have the past tense and the past participle the same; as,

Present.	Past.	Past Part.
Abide,	abode,	abode.
Sell,	sold,	sold.

3. Such as have the past tense and the past participle different; as,

Present.	Past.	Past Part.
Arise,	arose,	arisen.
Blow,	blew,	blown.

Many verbs become irregular by contraction; as, " feed, fed ; leave, left " : others, by the termination *en* ; as, " fall, fell, fallen " : others by the termination *ght ;* as " buy, bought ; teach, taught," &c.

5

LIST OF IRREGULAR VERBS.

Those Verbs which are conjugated regularly, as well as irregularly, are marked with an R.

Present.	Past.	Past Participle.
Abide	abode	abode
Am	was	been
Arise	arose	arisen
Awake	awoke R	awaked
Bear, *to bring forth*	bore, bare	born
Bear, *to carry*	bore, bare	borne
Beat	beat	beaten, *or* beat.
Begin	began	begun
Bend	bent R	bent
Bereave	bereft R	bereft R
Beseech	besought	besought
Bid, *for-*	bad, bade	bidden
Bind, *un-*	bound	bound
Bite	bit	bitten, bit
Bleed	bled	bled
Blow	blew	blown
Break	broke	broken
Breed	bred	bred
Bring	brought	brought
Build, *re-*	built *	built
Burst	burst	burst
Buy	bought	bought
Cast	cast	cast
Catch	caught R	caught R
Chide	chid	chidden, *or* chid
Choose	chose	chosen
Cleave, *to adhere*	clave R	cleaved
Cleave, *to split*	clove, *or* cleft	cloven, *or* cleft
Cling	clung	clung
Clothe	clothed	clad R
Come, *be-*	came	come
Cost	cost	cost
Crow	crew R	crowed
Creep	crept	crept
Cut	cut	cut
Dare, *to venture*	durst	dared
Dare, *to challenge is* R	dared	dared

* *Build, dwell,* and several other verbs, have the regular form, —*builded, dwelled,* etc.

Present.	Past.	Past Participle.
Deal	dealt R	dealt R
Dig	dug, or digged	dug, or digged
Do, mis- un- *	did	done
Draw, with-	drew	drawn
Drink	drank	drunk
Drive	drove	driven
Dwell	dwelt	dwelt R
Eat	ate	eaten
Fall, be-	fell	fallen
Feed	fed	fed
Feel	felt	felt
Fight	fought	fought
Find	found	found
Flee	fled	fled
Fling	flung	flung
Fly	flew	flown
Forbear	forbore	forborne
Forget	forgot	forgotten, forgot
Forsake	forsook	forsaken
Freeze	froze	frozen
Get, be- for-	got	got, gotten
Gild	gilt R	gilt R
Gird, be- en-	girt R	girt R
Give, for- mis-	gave	given
Go	went	gone
Grave, en-	graved	graven
Grind	ground	ground
Grow	grew	grown
Hang	hung	hung †
Have	had	had
Hear	heard	heard
Hew, rough-	hewed	hewn R
Hide	hid	hidden, or hid
Hit	hit	hit
Hold, be- with-	held	held
Hurt	hurt	hurt
Keep	kept	kept
Knit	knit R	knit, or knitted
Know	knew	known

* The compound verbs are conjugated like the simple Verbs, by prefixing the syllables appended to them: thus, Undo, undid, undone.

† Hang, to take away life by hanging, is regular; as, The robber was hanged, but the gown was hung up.

Present.	Past.	Past Participle.
Lade	laded	laden
Lay, in-	laid	laid
Lead, mis-	led	led
Leave	left	left
Lend	lent	lent
Let	let	let
Lie, to lie down	lay	lain
Load	loaded	laden R
Lose	lost	lost
Make	made	made
Mean	meant	meant
Meet	met	met
Mow	mowed	mown
Pay, re-	paid	paid
Put	put	put
Quit	quit, or quitted	quit R
Read	read	read
Rend	rent	rent
Rid	rid	rid
Ride	rode	ridden, or rode
Ring	rang, or rung	rung
Rise, a-	rose	risen
Rive	rived	riven
Run	ran	run
Saw	sawed	sawn R
Say	said	said
See	saw	seen
Seek	sought	sought
Seethe	seethed, or sod	sodden
Sell	sold	sold
Send	sent	sent
Set, be-	set	set
Shake	shook	shaken
Shape, mis-	shaped	shapen R
Shave	shaved	shaven R
Shear	shore R	shorn
Shed	shed	shed
Shine	shone R	shone R
Shoe	shod	shod
Shoot	shot	shot
Show	showed	shown
Shrink	shrank, or shrunk	shrunk
Shred	shred	shred

Present.	Past.	Past Participle.
Shut	shut	shut
Sing	sang, *or* sung	sung
Sink	sank, *or* sunk	sunk
Sit	sat	sat, *or* sitten
Slay	slew	slain
Sleep	slept	slept
Slide	slid	slidden
Sling	slang, *or* slung	slung
Slink	slank, *or* slunk	slunk
Slit	slit, *or* slitted	slit, *or* slitted
Smite	smote	smitten
Sow	sowed	sown R
Speak, *be-*	spoke, spake	spoken
Speed	sped	sped
Spend, *mis-*	spent	spent
Spill	spilt R	spilt R
Spin	span, *or* spun	spun
Spit, *be-*	spat, *or* spit	spitten, *or* spit
Split	split	split
Spread, *be-*	spread	spread
Spring	sprang, *or* sprung	sprung
Stand, *with-* &c.	stood	stood
Steal	stole	stolen
Stick	stuck	stuck
Sting	stung	stung
Stink	stank, *or* stunk	stunk
Stride, *be-*	strode, *or* strid	stridden
Strike	struck	struck, stricken
String	strang, *or* strung	strung
Strive	strove	striven
Strew, *be-*	strewed	strewed [ed
Strow	strowed	strown, *or* strow-
Swear	swore, *or* sware	sworn
Sweat	sweat	sweat
Sweep	swept	swept
Swell	swelled	swollen R
Swim	swam, *or* swum	swum
Swing	swang, *or* swung	swung
Take, *be-* &c.	took	taken
Teach, *mis- re-*	taught	taught
Tear, *un-*	tore	torn
Tell	told	told
Think, *be-*	thought	thought
Thrive	throve	thriven

Present.	Past.	Past Participle.
Throw	threw	thrown
Thrust	thrust	thrust
Tread	trod	trodden
Wax	waxed	waxen R
Wear	wore	worn
Weave	wove	woven
Weep	wept	wept
Win	won	won
Wind	wound	wound
Work	wrought R	wrought, worked
Wring	wrung	wrung
Write	wrote	written

DEFECTIVE VERBS

Are those which want some of their moods and tenses.

Present.	Past.	Past Participle.	Present.	Past.	Past Participle.
Can	could	———	Shall	should	———
May	might	———	Will	would	———
Must	must	———	Wis	wist	———
Ought	ought	———	Wit or Wot } wot		———
———	quoth	———			

PRETERITES AND PARTICIPLES.

In the preceding lists of Irregular Verbs, it will be observed that those Preterites and Participles which end in *t* are so formed in consequence of the *ed* being necessarily pronounced as a *t*, after certain letters, when it does not make a separate syllable.

Thus *keeped* has been changed into *kept*, *sleeped* into *slept*, *creeped* into *crept*, *kneeled* into *knelt*.

The *ed*, when the *e* is silent, has necessarily the sound of *t* after ch, k, p, sh, ss, or x; and hence *stretched*, *decked*, *lopped*, *hushed*, *tossed*, and *vexed*, are occasionally written with a terminal *t*, instead of the unpronounced *e* and the unpronounceable *d*.

The steps by which such changes are effected are easy and natural. The *e* was first left out by the poets lest the word should be mistaken for a dissyllable; and the substitution of *t* for *d* became afterwards a matter of course.

The words mentioned above, as well as others of the same class, appear in all the three modes of spelling, according to the pleasure of the author or printer:

stretched	stretch'd	strecht
decked	deck'd	deckt
lopped	lopp'd	lopt
hushed	hush'd	husht
tossed	toss'd	tost
vexed	vex'd	vext

Some grammarians introduce the terminations of *l*, *m*, *n*, as well as those already mentioned (*ch*, *k*, *p*, &c.), although the pronunciation of these terminal letters does not necessarily change the *d* into *t*.

deal	—	dealt	learn	—	learnt
dream	—	dreamt	mean	—	meant
lean	—	leant	burn	—	burnt

ADVERBS.

An Adverb is a part of Speech joined to a Verb, an Adjective, or another Adverb, to express some quality or circumstance of *time, place*, or *manner ;* as,

He reads WELL ;
He is a TRULY *good* man ;
He writes VERY *correctly.*

Some Adverbs are compared like Adjectives ; thus :

soon,	sooner,	soonest.
often,	oftener,	oftenest.

Those ending in *ly* are compared by *more* and *most*, and *less* and *least ;* as,

wisely,	more wisely,	most wisely.
justly,	more justly,	most justly.
justly,	less justly,	least justly.

Adverbs, though very numerous, are arranged in a few classes, the chief of which are these :

1. Number.	8. Comparison.
2. Order.	7. Quantity.
3. Place.	9. Affirmation.
4. Direction.	10. Negation.
5. Time.	11. Interrogation.
6. Quality or manner.	12. Doubt.

---

1. OF NUMBER.

Once,
Twice,
Thrice,
&c.

2. OF ORDER.

Firstly,	Fifthly,
Secondly,	Lastly,
Thirdly,	Finally,
Fourthly,	Ultimately.

---

3. OF PLACE.

Here,	Somewhere,	Thither,
There,	Nowhere,	Whence,
Where,	Herein,	Hence,
Elsewhere,	Whither,	Thence,
Anywhere,	Hither,	Whithersoever.

---

4. OF DIRECTION.

Upward,   Downward,   Backward,   Forward.

---

5. OF TIME.

Time Present.

Now,
To-day,
Presently,
Immediately.

Time Past.

Already,	Heretofore,
Before,	Hitherto,
Lately,	Long since,
Yesterday,	Long ago.

Time to come.	*Time Indefinite.*	
To-morrow,	Often,	Monthly,
Not yet,	Oftentimes,	Yearly,
Henceforth,	Oft-times,	Always,
Henceforward,	Sometimes,	Ever,
By and by,	Soon,	Never,
Shortly,	Seldom,	When,
Straitways,	Daily,	Then,
Hereafter.	Weekly,	Again, &c.

6. OF QUANTITY.

Much,	How great,
Little,	Abundantly,
Sufficiently,	Enough,
How much,	&c.

7. OF QUANTITY OR MANNER.

Wisely,	Unjustly,
Foolishly,	Quickly,
Justly,	Slowly.

Adverbs of this class are the most numerous; and they are generally formed by adding *ly* to an Adjective or Participle, or by changing *le* into *ly* ; as

Bad,	Badly,	Able,	Ably,
Cheerful,	Cheerfully.	Admirable,	Admirably.

8. OF COMPARISON.

More,	Worse,	Very,
Most,	Worst,	Almost,
Better,	Less,	Little,
Best,	Least,	Alike.

9. OF AFFIRMATION.

Verily,	Yea,
Truly,	Yes,
Undoubtedly,	Surely,
Doubtless,	Indeed,
Certainly,	Really, &c.

---

10. OF NEGATION.

Nay,	By no means,
No,	Not at all,
Not,	In no wise, &c.

---

11. OF INTERROGATION.

How,	Wherefore,
Why,	Whither, &c.

---

12. OF DOUBT.

Perhaps,	Possibly,
Peradventure,	Perchance.

NOTE.—For further Illustrations, and an Improved Definition of the Adverb, see p. 94.

PREPOSITIONS.

Prepositions are used to connect words with one another, and to show the relation between them. They are mostly put before Nouns and Pronouns. For example :

He went *from* London *to* York ;
She is *above* disguise ;
They are supported *by* industry.

The following is a list of the principal Preposition.—Commit them to memory, and you will soon be able to distinguish them from the other Parts of Speech :

of	under	up	unto
to	through	down	across
for	above	before	around
by	below	behind	amidst
with	between	off	throughout
in	beneath	on *or* upon	underneath
into	from	among	betwixt
within	beyond	after	beside
without	at	about	towards
over	near	against	notwithstanding

Prepositions, in their original and literal acceptation, seem to have denoted relations of place; but they are now used *figuratively* to express other relations. For example, as persons who are *above* have in several respects the advantage of such as are *below*, so Prepositions expressing high and low places are used for superiority and inferiority in general : as, " He is *above* disguise"; " We serve *under* a good master "; " He rules *over* a willing people "; " We should do nothing *beneath* our character."

Some of the Prepositions have the appearance and effect of Conjunctions: as, " *After* their prisons were thrown open," &c.; " *Before* I die"; " They made haste to be prepared *against* their friends arrived" : but if the noun *time*, which is understood, be added, they will lose their conjunctive form ; as, " After [the time when] their prisons," &c.

The Prepositions *after, before, above, beneath,* and several others, sometimes appear to be Adverbs and may be so considered : as, "They had their reward soon *after*"; "He died not long *before*"; "He dwells *above*": but if the Nouns *time* and *place* be added, they will lose their adverbial form; as, "He died not long *before that time*," &c.

CONJUNCTIONS.

A Conjunction is a part of speech that is chiefly used to connect sentences; so as, out of two or more sentences, to make but one. It sometimes connects only words.

Conjunctions are principally divided into two sorts,—the Copulative and the Disjunctive.

The Conjunction Copulative serves to connect or to continue a sentence, by expressing an addition, a supposition, a cause, &c. : as, "He *and* his brother reside in London"; "I will go *if* he will accompany me"; "You are happy, *because* you are good."

The Conjunction Disjunctive serves, not only to connect and continue the sentence, but also to express opposition of meaning in different degrees : as, "*Though* he was frequently reproved, *yet* he did not reform"; "They came with her, *but* they went away without her."

The following are the principal Conjunctions, which may easily be committed to memory :

COPULATIVE CONJUNCTIONS.

and,	them,	therefore,
if,	since,	wherefore,
that,	for,	provided,
both,	because,	besides.

but,	however,	notwithstanding,
or,	otherwise,	nevertheless,
nor,	unless,	except,
than,	either,	whether,
lest,	neither,	whereas,
though,	yet,	as well as.

Some Conjunctions are followed by similar Conjunctions, so that the latter answers to the former. For example :—

Though is followed by *yet :*

Though he was not strong, *yet* he was industrious.

Either is followed by *or :*

I will *either* send it, *or* bring it myself.

Neither is followed by *nor :*

Neither John *nor* James can speak French.

As is followed by *as :*

She is *as* diligent *as* her sister.

As is followed by *so :*

As the sapling is, *so* will be the oak.

INTERJECTIONS.

Interjections are words thrown-in between the parts of a sentence to express the passions or emotions of the speaker; as,

Oh! I have alienated my friend.

Alas! I fear he is lost.

O Virtue, how amiable thou art!

The following are the principal Interjections:

Ah! Ah me! Aha! Alas! Alack! Away!
Begone! Bravo! Dear me! Eh! Fie! Ha!
Halloo! Hurra! Hush! Lo! O! Oh!
Oh dear! Pooh! Pshaw! Tush!

PART THIRD.

Section I.

ILLUSTRATIONS OF THE PARTS OF SPEECH.

A GENERAL VIEW OF THE PARTS OF SPEECH.

To be committed to Memory.

1. A SUBSTANTIVE or Noun is the name of anything that exists, or of which we have any notion; as London, man, virtue.

A Substantive may, in general, be known by its taking an Article before it, or by its making sense of itself: as, a *book*, the *sun*, an *apple;* temperance, industry, honesty.

The Abstract Nouns (which are the most difficult) may easily be known by placing them either before or after *another* Noun in the Possessive Case. For example :

The man's *strength*, or the *strength* of the man.
The woman's *industry*, or the *industry* of the woman.
The child's *health*, or the *health* of the child.
The fox's *cunning*, or the *cunning* of the fox.
The elephant's *sagacity*, or the *sagacity* of the elephant.
The tiger's *ferocity*, or the *ferocity* of the tiger.

2. An ADJECTIVE is a word added to a Substantive to express its quality; as, an *industrious* man, a *virtuous* woman.

An Adjective may be known by its making sense with the addition of the word *thing;* as, a *good* thing, a *bad* thing. Or it may be known by its making sense with any particular Substantive as, a *sweet* apple, a *pleasant* prospect, a *lively* boy.

3. An ARTICLE is a word prefixed to Substantives, to point them out, and to show how far their signification extends; as *a* garden, *an* eagle, *the* woman.

The Articles (being only *three*) can never be forgotten.

The Indefinite Article is *A* when used before words beginning with a *consonant;* as

a book, a map, a tree :

but it is *AN* when used before words beginning with a *vowel* or a *silent h;* as

an acorn, an hour.

When the *h* is *sounded*, the *a* only is used ; as

a hand, a heart, a highway.

NOTE.—*A* must be used before words beginning with U long (which is, in reality, a *consonantal sound*) ; as, a university, a union, a useful book : and *an* only before words beginning with U short; as, *an* uproar, *an* usher, *an* umbrella.

The peculiar use and importance of the articles will be seen in the following examples:

1. The son of the king.
2. A son of the king.
3. The son of a king.
4. A son of a king.

Each of these phrases has an entirely different meaning, in consequence of the different application of the Articles *a* and *the*.

4. A PRONOUN is a word used instead of a Noun, to avoid the too-frequent repetition of the same word; as, the man is happy, *he* is benevolent, *he* is useful.

The Pronouns are not numerous, and must be all committed to memory. (See page 38.)

5. A VERB is a word which signifies to *Be*, to *Do*, or to *Suffer*; as, I *am*, I *rule*, I *am ruled*.

A Verb may generally be distinguished by its making sense with any of the Personal Pronouns, or the word *to* before it: as, I *walk*, he *plays*, they *write*; or to *walk*, to *play*, to *write*.

6. An ADVERB is a part of speech joined to a Verb, an Adjective, and sometimes to another Adverb, to express some quality or circumstance respecting it: as, He reads *well*; a *truly* good man; he writes *very* correctly.

An Adverb may be generally known by its answering to the questions, How? How much? When? or Where?—as in the phrase, He reads *correctly*, the answer to the question, How does he read? is *correctly*.

7. PREPOSITIONS serve to connect words with one another, and to show the relation between them: as, He went *from* London *to* York; She is *above* disguise; They are supported *by* industry.

A Preposition may be known by its admitting after it a Personal Pronoun in the objective case. Thus, *with*, *for*, *to*, &c. will allow the objective case after them; as with *him*, for *her*, to *them*, &c.

The whole of the Prepositions must be committed to memory. (See page 75.)

8. A CONJUNCTION is a part of Speech that is chiefly used to connect sentences; so as, out of two or more sentences, to make but one: it sometimes connects only words: as, Thou and he are happy, *because* you are good; Two *and* three are five.

The principal Conjunctions must be committed to memory. (See pages 76 and 77.)

9. An INTERJECTION is a word used to express some passion or emotion of the mind: as, Oh! I have alienated my friend; alas! I fear for life.

It will be impossible to make any mistake about the Interjections.

NOTE.—The observations here made to help the learners in distinguishing the parts of speech from one another, may afford them some small assistance in their first exercises; but it will certainly be much more instructive to learn to distinguish them by their definitions, and by an accurate knowledge of their nature.

In the following passage, all the Parts of Speech are exhibited:

3   1   7   1   5 3   1   2   7 1
The power of speech is a faculty peculiar to man;

5   5   7 4 7 4   2   1
and was bestowed on him, by his beneficent Creator,

7 3   2   8   6   2   1   8 9
for the greatest and most excellent uses; but, alas!

6 6 5 4   5 4 7 3 2 7   1
how often do we pervert it to the worst of purposes!

A BRIEF SUMMARY OF THE PARTS OF SPEECH.

1. *Nouns* or *Substantives,*	{ Names of persons, places, & things. Names of Qualities and Actions.
2. *Adjectives,*	Express the Qualities of Nouns.
3. *Articles* (*The, An, A*),	Indicate Nouns.
4. *Pronouns,*	Words used instead of Nouns.
5. *Verbs,*	Signify to Be,—to Do,—to Be Done to.
6. *Adverbs,*	{ Express the quality of Verbs. Express the quality of Adjectives. Some Adverbs qualify other Adverbs.
7. *Prepositions,* ..	Show the Relation of Nouns and Pronouns to each other.
8. *Conjunctions,* ..	Connect sentences, phrases, and words.
9. *Interjections,* ..	Sudden Expressions of Surprise Pleasure, Pain, or Disgust.

6

Section II.

ILLUSTRATIONS OF ETYMOLOGICAL PARSING.

[With numerous Exercises.]

The following illustrations of the First Rule of Syntax are here introduced, because it is impossible to parse a Verb without referring to the agreement which must be maintained between the Verb and its Nominative.

The pupil must therefore learn, and thoroughly understand, that

A Verb must agree with its Nominative in Number and Person.

There are three persons singular, and three persons plural.

First Person Singular,........*I* learn.
Second Person Singular,......*Thou* learnest.
Third Person Singular,.......*He* learns.

First Person Plural, ...*We* learn.
Second Person Plural, ...*You* learn.
Third Person Plural,.........*They* learn.

In the first person singular, *I* is the Nominative to the Verb *learn.*

In the second person singular, *Thou* is the Nominative to the Verb *learnest.*

In the third person singular, *He* is the Nominative to the Verb *learns.*

And so on of the others.

A Verb must agree with its Nominative in Number and Person.

Singular Number.	Plural Number.
The boy runs.	The boys run.
The girl walks.	The girls walk.

Here the Verb agrees with its Nominative in *Number.*

When the Noun or Pronoun which is the Nominative, is in the singular number, the Verb which agrees with it is also said to be in the singular number.

When the Noun or Pronoun which is the Nominative, is in the plural number, the Verb which agrees with it is also said to be in the plural number.

First Person,.............I read.
Second Person,...........Thou readest.
Third Person, ...He reads.

Here the Verb agrees with its Nominative in *Person.*

When the Noun or Pronoun which is the Nominative, is in the first person, the Verb which agrees with is also said to be in the first person.

When the Noun or Pronoun which is the Nominative, is in the second person, the Verb which agrees with it is also said to be in the second person.

When the Noun or Pronoun which is the Nominative, is in the third person, the Verb which agrees with it is also said to be in the third person.

A Verb must agree with its Nominative in Number and Person.

QUESTIONS FOR ETYMOLOGICAL PARSING.

What part of speech.

1. A Noun.
{ Common or proper? What Gender? Number? Case? Why?

2. An Adjective.
{ Why an Adjective? To what does it belong? What degree of comparison?

3. An Article.   What kind? Why?

4. A Pronoun.
{ What kind? Person? Gender? Number? Case? Why?

5. A Verb.
{ What kind? Mood? Tense? Number? Person? Why? If a Participle? Why? Active or Passive? Why?

6. An Adverb.
{ Why is it an Adverb? Does it qualify a Verb? or an Adjective? or another Adverb?

7. A Preposition.   Why?

8. A Conjunction.   What kind? Why?

9. An Interjection.   Why?

SPECIMENS OF ETYMOLOGICAL PARSING.

John's hand trembles.

John's—   is a Noun, because it is the name of a person.

It is a Proper Noun, because it is the name of an individual.

It is masculine, because it denotes a male.

It is in the third person, because it is spoken of.

It is of the singular number, because it means only one.

It is in the possessive case, because it signifies possession.

Hand— is a Noun, because it is the name of a thing.

It is a Common Noun, because it is the name of a sort, or kind, or species of thing.

It is of the neuter gender, because it is neither male nor female.

It is in the third person, because it is spoken of.

It is in the singular number, because it means but one.

It is in the nominative case, because it is the actor and subject of the Verb " Trembles."

*Trembles—*is a Verb, because it is a word which signifies to do.

It is an Active Verb, because it expresses action.

It is in the third person, because it agrees with "hand," which is in the third person.

It is in the singular number, because it agrees with "hand," which is in the singular number.

NOTE.—The first eight or ten sentences of the Parsing Exercises should be done according to the above Model; but afterwards they might be done according to the following briefer method:

They who forgive, act nobly.

*They—*is a Personal Pronoun, nominative case.— (*Decline it.*)

*Who—*is a Relative Pronoun, nominative case.—(*Decline it.*)

*Forgive—*is an Irregular Verb Active, indicative mood, present tense, and the third person plural. (*Repeat the present tense, the imperfect tense, and the perfect participle.*)

*Act—*is a Regular Verb Active, indicative mood, present tense, and the third person plural. (*Repeat the subjunctive mood and the participles.*)

*Nobly—*is an Adverb of Quality. (*Repeat the degrees of comparison.*)

By living temperately, our health is promoted.

By—is a Preposition.

Living—is the present participle of the Regular Neuter Verb " *To Live.*" (*Conjugate the Verb.*)

Temperately—is an Adverb of Quality.

Our—is an Adjective Pronoun of the possessive kind.

Health—is a Common Substantive, of the third person, the singular number, and in the nominative case.— (*Decline it.*)

Is promoted—is a Regular Verb Passive, indicative mood, present tense, and the third person singular. (*Repeat the potential mood and the participles.*)

We should be kind to them who are unkind to us.

We—is a Personal Pronoun, of the first person, the plural number, and in the nominative case.— (*Decline it.*)

Should be—is an Irregular Verb Neuter, in the potential mood, the imperfect tense, and the first person plural. (*Repeat the indicative mood and the participles.*)

Kind—is an Adjective in the positive state. (*Repeat the degrees of comparison.*)

To—is a Preposition.

Them—is a Personal Pronoun, of the third person, the plural number, and in the objective case.— (*Decline it.*)

Who—is a Relative Pronoun, in the nominative case.— (*Decline it.*)

Are—is an Irregular Verb Neuter, indicative mood, present tense, and the third person plural. (*Repeat the potential mood and the participles.*)

Unkind—is an Adjective in the positive state. (*Repeat the degrees of comparison.*)

To—is a Preposition.

Us—is a Personal Pronoun of the first person, the plural number, and in the objective case.— (*Decline it.*)

Parsing Exercises on Nouns, Adjectives, and Articles.

A winding canal.
An affectionate parent.
A melancholy fact.
An interesting history.
A happy life.
The woodbine's fragrance.
A cheering prospect.
An harmonious sound.
Delicious fruit.
The sweetest incense.
An odorous garden.
The sensitive plant.
A convenient mansion.
Warm clothing.
A temperate climate.
Wholesome aliment.

A garden enclosed.
The ivy-mantled tower.
Virtue's fair form.
A mahogany table.
Sweet-scented myrtle.
A resolution wise, noble, disinterested.
Consolation's lenient hand.
A better world.
A cheerful, good old man.
A silver tea-urn.
Tender-looking charity.
My brother's wife's mother.
A book of my friends.
An animating, well-founded hope.

Parsing Exercises on Pronouns, Verbs, &c.

I am sincere.
Thou art industrious.
He is disinterested.
We honour them.
You encourage us.
They command her.
Thou dost improve.
He assisted me.
We completed our journey.
Our hopes did flatter us.
They have deceived me.

Let us improve ourselves.
Know yourselves.
Let them advance.
They may offend.
I can forgive.
He might surpass them.
We could overtake him.
I would be happy.
Ye should repent.
He may have deceived me.
They may have forgotten.

Parsing Exercises on Adverbs, Prepositions, and Conjunctions.

I have seen him once, perhaps twice.
Thirdly, and lastly, I shall conclude.
This plant is found here, and elsewhere.
Only to-day is properly ours.
The task is already performed.

We could not serve him then, but we will hereafter.
We often resolve, but seldom perform.
He is much more promising now than formerly.
We are wisely and happily directed.

Mentally and bodily, we are curiously and wonderfully formed.

By diligence and frugality, we arrive at competency.

We are often below our wishes, and above our deserts.

From virtue to vice, the progress is gradual.

We in vain look for a path between virtue and vice.

Some things make for him, others against him.

By this imprudence, he was plunged into new difficulties.

Without the aid of charity, he supported himself with credit.

Parsing Exercises on the same word used as different Parts of Speech.

Some words, from the different ways in which they are used, belong sometimes to one Part of Speech, sometimes to another.

EXAMPLES.

As is sometimes used as a relative Pronoun, sometimes as an Adverb: as, Let me have such a reward *as* I deserve; Give him *as* much *as* he desires.

BUT is sometimes used as a Preposition, sometimes as a Conjunction: as, Nothing *but* temperance will preserve health; I live in Montreal, *but* my brother lives in Quebec.

EITHER and NEITHER are used both as Numeral Adjectives and as Conjunctions: as, I will take *either* of them; *either* speak the truth or keep silent.

MUCH, MORE, and MOST are used both as Adjectives and as Adverbs: as, In *most* towns *much* money has been collected; but *more* ought to have been collected.—*Most* certainly; but I am *much* gratified by what I have got,—the *more* so as I did not expect it.

THIS and THAT are not always Pronouns. When I say, "I shall eat *this* apple (or *that* apple)," it is clear that the word *this* (or *that*) placed before the word "apple," does not stand instead of any Noun mentioned before, or understood; therefore it is not a Pronoun. It stands in the place of an Article or an Adjective, and performs precisely the same duty; and consequently in all such cases it must be regarded as an Article or an Adjective.

THAT is used as a Numeral Adjective, a Relative Pronoun, and a Conjunction: as, I will thank you for *that* book; I will thank you for the book *that* is beside you; I beg *that* you will hand me the book.

Calm was the day, and the scene delightful.

We may expect a calm after a storm.

To prevent passion, is easier than to calm it

The gay and the dissolute think little of the miseries which are stealing softly after them.

A little attention will rectify some errors.

Better is a little with content, than a great deal with anxiety.

Though he is out of danger, he is still afraid.

He laboured to still the tumult.

Still waters are commonly the deepest.

Damp air is unwholsome.

Guilt often casts a damp over our sprightliest hours.

Soft bodies damp the sound much more than hard ones.

Though she is rich and fair, yet she is not aimable.

They are yet young, and must suspend their judgment yet awhile.

Many persons are better than we suppose them to be.

The few and the many have their prepossessions.

Few days pass without some clouds.

The desire of getting more, is rarely satisfied.

He has equal knowledge, but inferior judgment.

She is his inferior in sense, but his equal in prudence.

Every being loves its like.

Behave yourselves like men

We are too apt to like pernicious company.

He may go or stay, as he likes.

They strive to learn.

He goes to and fro.

To his wisdom we owe our privilege.

The proportion is ten to one.

He has served them with his utmost ability.

When we do our utmost, no more is required.

I will submit, for I know it brings peace.

It is for our health to be temperate.

O! for better times.

I have a regard for him.

Promiscuous Exercises in Etymological Parsing.

Engrave on your minds this sacred rule : "Do unto others, as you wish that they should do unto you."

Truth and candour possess a powerful charm : they bespeak universal favor.

Of what small moment to our real happiness, are many of those injuries which draw forth our resentment!

Opportunities occur daily for strengthening in ourselves the habits of virtue.

They who are learning to compose and arrange their sentences with accuracy and order, are learning at the same time to think with accuracy and order.

Section III.

ANALYTICAL ILLUSTRATIONS.

ADJECTIVES AND PARTICIPLES.

Nouns are changeable into Verbs, and Verbs into Nouns. Things may become active, and the names of actions may be considered abstractedly so as to lose the idea of activity. The Infinitive is purely a Noun; and to produce what the Noun designates, is as certainly a Verb.

Adjectives and Participles stand in a similar relationship. They are both qualities : but when the quality is quiescent, it is termed an Adjective ; and when it relates to action, or to a state of existence which may be conceived as variable, it is a Participle.

Participles are compound words, expressing the *quality* of being the *agent* or the *object* of an action : and they must also be considered as Adjectives which owe their verbal signification to their affixes ; as *loving* and *drowned* are formed by the *active* addition of *ing* and *ed.*

Participles are like Verbs when they express action and being, and refer to time present and to time past; and they are like Adjectives when they refer to Nouns, and explain their action and being.

When either the present or the perfect Participle is placed before a Noun, it becomes a describing or explaining Adjective ; as

A *loving* companion.   The *roaring* winds.
The *flowing* stream.   An *accomplished* scholar.

Here the words *loving, flowing, roaring, accomplished,* describe or explain the quality of the Nouns with which they are placed.

The following examples will fully explain the double nature of this class of words :

> His writings are much to be *admired.*
> He is an *admired* writer.
> They were *admiring* her singing.
> He sang to an *admiring* audience.
> He is *amusing* his friends with an *amusing* story.

See the sun *setting !*	See the *setting* sun!
See the moon *rising !*	See the *rising* moon
The wind is *roaring.*	Hear the *roaring* wind!
The twig is *broken.*	The *broken* twig fell.

When Participles are used as Adjectives, they are called *Participial Adjectives.*

CLASSIFICATION OF VERBS.

NOTE.—Besides the divisions of Verbs which have already been explained (see page 49), there is another important division of Verbs to which the pupil's attention may now be directed ; and that is into *Transitive* and *Intransitive.*

VERBS—TRANSITIVE AND INTRANSITIVE.

The word *Transitive* means *passing over*, and the word *Intransitive* means *not passing over.*

A *Transitive* Verb expresses an act done by one person or thing to another person or thing ; as, John *strikes* the horse, the horse *kicks* John.

The Verb active is called *Transitive* because the action *passes over* to the object, or has an effect upon some other thing ; as, the tutor *instructs* his pupils, I esteem the man.

An *Intransitive* Verb expresses *the being* or *state* of its subject (or nominative). An Intransitive Verb expresses an act *not* done to another person or thing ; as, I *am*, they *sleep*, he *runs.*

Verbs Neuter may properly be denominated *Intransitive*, because the effect is confined within the subject ; as, I *sit*, he *lives*, they *walk.*

These two classes of Verbs may be thus designated:

1.—*Transitive* Verbs in the Active Voice require an object after them to complete the sense; as, John *strikes* the *horse*.

Intransitive Verbs do not require an object after them, but the sense is complete without it; as, he *sits*, you *ride*, the wind *blows*, the wheel *turns*.

2.—As the object of a Transitive Active Verb is in the objective case, any Verb which makes sense with *me, him, her, it, then*, after it, is Transitive. A Verb that does not make sense with one of these words after it, is Intransitive: thus, *strikes* is Transitive, because we can say John strikes *me*; *sleeps* is Intransitive, because we cannot say John sleeps *me*.

When a Verb in the active voice has an object, it is *Transitive*; when it has not an object, it is *Intransitive*.

3.—In the use of *Transitive* Verbs, three things are always understood,—the *actor*, the *act*, and the *object* acted upon. In the use of *Intransitive* Verbs, there are only two things understood,—the *subject*, and the *being*, or *state*, or *act*, of the subject.

THE IMPERATIVE MOOD.

The Imperative Mood is used for *commanding, exhorting, entreating*, or *permitting*; as,

Let *me* study.	Let *us* study.
Study *thou* or do *thou* study.	Study *you* or do *you* study.
Let *him* study.	Let *them* study.

In these six sentences we appear to have the three persons singular and the three persons plural of the Pronouns and Verbs; but on a careful examination it will easily be perceived, that each sentence is, in fact, *an address to* one or more persons,—that they all imply a person or persons *spoken to*,—and that therefore they are all in the SECOND *Person* Singular or Plural.

Whenever we *command, exhort, entreat,* or *permit,* we speak TO one or more persons; and as the person or persons *spoken* TO are always in the *second* person, *the Imperative Mood can only be used in the Second Person.*

" Let *me* study," means " Do thou (or you) allow *me* to study."

" Let *him* study," means " Do thou (or you) allow *him* to study."

" Let *us* study," means " Do thou (or you) allow *us* to study."

" Let *them* study," means " Do thou (or you) allow *them* to study."

And so on, of all other phrases which can be used in the Imperative Mood,—merely modified to suit the variations of command, exhortation, entreaty, or permission, but always in the *second person.*

PROGRESSIVE AND EMPHATIC FORM OF VERBS.

An Active or a Neuter Verb may be conjugated through all its moods and tenses, by adding the *present participle* to the Verb To Be.

This is called the *Progressive* Form, because it expresses the continuation of action or state ; as,

Present.	*Past.*
I am loving.	I was loving.
Thou art loving.	Thou wast loving.
He is loving, &c.	He was loving, &c.

The present and the past Indicative are also conjugated by the Auxiliaries *Do* and *Did,* which is called the *Emphatic* Form ; as,

Present.	*Past.*
I do love.	I did love.
Thou dost love.	Thou didst love.
He does love, &c.	He did love, &c.

ADVERBS MODIFY PREPOSITIONS.

It has been already repeated, that An Adverb is a word joined to a Verb, an Adjective, and sometimes to another Adverb, to express some quality or circumstance respecting it. But besides these relations which the Adverb has respectively with the *Verb, Adjective*, or with another *Adverb*, it has also a relation with the *Preposition*, as may be seen in the following 'examples :

I have had too MUCH *of* that.

I must have MORE *of* this.

I only wish to have ENOUGH *of* every thing.

He lives CONSIDERABLY *above* his means.

He has ENOUGH *for* his present wants.

John is NEARLY *up* to James in his Latin.

His head was QUITE *under* the water.

The water is SCARCELY *below* its usual level.

He went ALMOST *to* Quebec.

Improved Definition of the Adverb.

An Adverb is a word joined to a *Verb*, an *Adjective*, a *Preposition*, or another *Adverb*, to modify it, or to denote some circumstance respecting it : as, "Fred *learns* WELL ; he is REMARKABLY *diligent ;* he has advanced CONSIDERABLY *beyond* his class-mates ; and he draws VERY *beautifully*."

Phrases which do the duty of Adverbs, are termed Adverbial Phrases : as, " in the best manner possible ; in fine ; in general ; in vain ; at most ; at least ; so on ; such like," &c.

ORIGIN OF ADVERBS.

The *quality* of a Noun is expressed by an Adjective, and the *state* of a Noun is expressed by a Verb; but the former admits of degrees, and the latter of modifications: a substance may be more or less white, and an action may be more or less violent.

The modification of Verbs is, however, much more varied than that of Adjectives: it is dependent on different circumstances, such as *time, place, manner,* &c.; which circumstances may be expressed, in every instance, by means of a Subtantive and a Preposition.

" He struck the ball," records a simple act; but " He struck the ball *with force,*" gives a qualification to the Verb.

" They treated him *with kindness* " (or *in a kind manner*), " I shall see him *in a short time,*" are examples of a similar kind.

The modifications produced by the relations of *time, place, manner,* &c., are so frequent, that the short clauses of adverbial phrases are constantly recurring. Repetition naturally induces hasty pronunciation and consequent contraction. The phrase is gradually curtailed, by leaving something to be understood; and its remaining parts are, at last, compressed into a single word, which is then termed an Adverb.

In the above examples, the clauses " *with force* ' " *with kindness,*" and " *in a short time,*" may be equally well expressed by the Adverbs *forcibly, kindly,* and *soon.*

The far greater part of Adverbs, in all languages, answer to the question—How, or in what manner, a state exists, or an action is performed ?

These modes of existence, or of actions, being qualities, must have a similitude to Adjectives; and accordingly, they differ in English, in most cases, merely by the addition of *ly,* signifying *like :*—thus a *prudent* man acts *prudently,* and a *wise* man acts *wisely.*

There are nearly three thousand words which are marked as Adverbs in the latest editions of English Dictionaries, of which about three fourths terminate in *ly.*

W and Y are ALWAYS *Vowels.*

W has the power of *oo*, the sound heard in the word good; and at the beginning of words or syllables, it always forms a regular diphthong with the vowel which immediately follows; as in

way,	which is sounded	ŏŏay.
water,	" "	ŏŏa-ter.
went,	" "	ŏŏent.
win,	" "	ŏŏin.
bewilder,	" "	be-ŏŏil-der.

And so on in every case in which it begins a word or syllable. And when it is not at the beginning of a word or syllable, it also invariably coalesces with the succeeding vowel and forms a regular diphthong; as in

twin,	which is sounded	tŏŏin.
twenty,	" "	tŏŏen-ty
twist,	" "	tŏŏist.

W is silent in the irregular diphthongs *wo* and *ow*; as in *two, tow,* &c.

Y has the power of *e,* as in beauty; or of *i,* as in by.

Y, when it begins a word or syllable, is always pure *e,* uttered in an abrupt manner or pronoṇ .ced quickly, and invariably coalesces with the succeeding v .wel to form a diphthong; as in

yesterday,	which ı sounded	čes-ter-day.
you,	" "	ēoo.
yoke,	" "	čoke.
bowyer,	" "	bow-ēer.

And so on in every case in which it begins a word or syllable. At the end of a word or syllable,—or when it is at neither extremity of a word or syllable, as in *myrrh,*—or when it forms a syllable of itself, as in dew-*y,*—it is either lost in the preceding vowel, or has the precise function which would be possessed in the same case by the vowel *i.*

THE END.

www.ingramcontent.com/pod-product-compliance
Lightning Source LLC
Chambersburg PA
CBHW020026030726
47499CB00007B/2299